SETTI

OUT TO

DECEIVE?

A Tale of Two

Sisters

>>>>><<<<<

PETUNIA PLANT

SETTING OUT TO DECEIVE ?

ISBN : 978-0-993-4644-6-1

© Petunia Plant

April 2022

NETHERMOOR BOOKS

"St. Elphin,"

12 North Promenade

Withernsea

HU19 2DP

Telephone : 01964-615258

Author Petunia Plant is contactable via her Publisher or her Agent

>>>><<<<

Dedicated

to all

my Teachers

at

Withernsea

High School

>>>><<<<

<< The Grass is not, in fact,

always greener on the

other side of the Fence.

Not at all.

Fences have nothing

to do with it.

The Grass is greenest

when it is watered.

When crossing over Fences:

carry water with you;

and tend the grass

wherever you may be. >>

[Erma Bombeck 1927-1996]

SETTING OUT TO DECEIVE ?

A TALE OF TWO SISTERS

---

the year is
2002

ONE :

"Let's swop!" was Candida's suggestion.

"Yes: *swop*! " agreed Ophelia, impishly.

It was a lazy Saturday morning when these two sisters started to put the building blocks of their plan in place.

"You have Nev - and I'll have Steve !" proposed Candida.... *"for one night only!"*

"One night only!" echoed Ophelia: "a sort of one night stand!"

"You could say that!" responded the younger sister, with unrestrained glee.

There followed a few minutes' silence : both girls immersed in some of their mother's discarded CHAT Magazines. A good excuse for postponing any residual Homework.

"Odd choice for her: CHAT!" Candida commented.

"S'pose it's the Real-Life that hooks her?" Ophelia speculated, "*See how the other half lives?*"

At this stage of Upper School Candida was seeing more of her Nev than Ophelia, Steve. Because Neville, as he didn't want to be known as went to the same School, albeit in 11E, not 11P, and doing different GCSEs. "Yes *you* have Nev and *I'll* have Steve!" Candida confirmed.

It sounded better the more she said it. Quite decisive when put so baldly.

Then, despite her initial enthusiasm, Ophelia found doubt creeping in. Lounging on her bed, almost flat on her back, she suggested Candida was getting the better deal.

"You know Steve's rich? *Seriously* rich!"

Candida, unimpressed, reacted: "Jammy! That would p'raps explain why you were dumbstruck in the first place!"

"I *wasn't* awestruck as you put it so crudely; nor was he initially taken by *me*!" protested Ophelia: " I'd have liked him even if he'd been penniless. Penniless!"

"I'm sure ! I mean, I'm *not* sure ! I'm not sure you'd ever go out with somebody in rags..." checked out the younger sister.

"Maybe. Maybe not. Anyway I hate the way you talk about *rags*. Next you'll be suggesting Nev goes round in rags: a ragged-trousered something-or-other....Ooops! I don't think that was very...." Here the older girl hesitated.

Nor did she get chance to end her sentence - as Sis had discovered a pressing need to use the *en suite*. With the door closed.

"Nev's not *totally* without, you know! Candida explained upon her reappearance. "It's just he wasn't born with a silver spoon in his mouth. He's only *a bit* hard up, and only for some of the time. *You'll* see!"

"I'll both see - and won't be *bothered* what I see," announced Ophelia quite decisively. "And if he *does* turn up with no silver spoon in his mouth, I'll take it that it dropped out whilst he was saying sweet nothings to *you*!"

"That's enough! The swop's off! I'm not having you - *of all people* - making a fool of Neville!" responded Candida, indignantly.

Sighing, the younger girl made a great show of getting such an authoritative text as: '*The English Midlands*' out of her school-bag; jotting down some sparse notes ready for Geography on Monday.

"You've got the better deal, *whatever* happens! The best cut of the beast!" Ophelia had evidently decided to stick to butcher's lingo: knowing full well her semi-vegetarian sister would be revolted by *any* person being compared to a choice fillet steak. Then she conceded: "But I s'pose it's okay for *one night only*...."

"You mean you won't be kept in the manner to which you are accustomed !" Candida retorted.

"*Lay off* ! You still believe I've gone for a man for his money?" Ophelia objected.

"Well you've never exactly gone *without*!"

"I have and I *do*," protested Ophelia: "When I went out with Callum, all he did was tramp, tramp, tramp. It turned out he was a fanatical Rambler who only wanted to take me for walks! In the open countryside! And *more* walks! Walking was what he did !"

"And that's why there's no more *Callum*! Liquidated ! Expunged! Sent packing! A non-person : all because big Sis' shoes wore out!"

This time it was Candida who had gone too far. Ophelia swiped her with a cushion: once, twice, thrice - and *not* for fun! In response to which attack the younger girl did nothing except giggle.... and shield her head: quite *ostentatiously,* shielding her head.

TWO :

"For one night only!" Ophelia stressed, when the two girls picked up their daring plan and ran with it later that morning : *"for one night only- I warn you!"*

"Don't make it so obvious you can only stand Nev for a couple of hours! What does that say about *me* ?" objected Candida.

"Only *you* can know that, know what *you* want, Candy: discover your Heart's Desire in the wake of Alfie," was Ophelia's assessment as she attempted to digest some more Anatomy for Biology 'A' Level. "But we'll have to be *everso* careful? Any visible hole in our plan and we're sunk: *drowneded*!"

"Holes aren't visible - or else there wouldn't be holes," quipped Candida, "if you see what I mean?"

"Clever-clogs! Too clever!" answered the older sister, "and anyway most holes *are* visible; it's just nobody does anything about them!"

"You mean we're con*demned* to be rumbled?"

"Rumbled, *and ridiculed*: if you ask me! That's what I predict," was Ophelia's grim assessment.

"Wrecked!?" exclaimed Candida.

"Beached - *and* with *egg* on our faces," Ophelia added.

"Yes I'm afraid it's curtains down if it all goes up like a balloon!" Candida agreed, whilst still not sure how she'd chosen balloon taking off - balloon bursting? - in preference to 'pear-shaped.' "Tell nobody *nothing*!"

"You mean tell nobody *anything* - or tell anybody nothing?" Here the older sister was correcting the younger sister's grammar.

"Nothing! Our lips are *sealed*!" Candida promised.

The two sisters *would have* planned longer except for Mum breezing in with a jug of coffee, *without knocking*.

"You're *supposed* to knock!" cried Ophelia with mock exasperation.

"Sorry, Madam! Couldn't ! Tray in my hand! I'll take it away!" the girls' mother offered without meaning it.

"You might have found one of us *naked!*" joked Candida.

"Well that wouldn't be the first time - nor the last! You were born naked! And one day you might catch *me* naked!" Mum foresaw.

"God I hope not!" gasped Candida.
"Thanks for the Coffee! Much better half-milk," Ophelia interjected : "but I'm sure you want something *of us*?"

"Yes I do!" Mum affirmed : "it's a glorious morning for September, and I want to see all your pants and pyjamas on the line, not in the lin-bin.... and your *Saturday* job is to clean the kitchen, *including* the floor."

"But it *is* clean ! *Everso* clean !" Candida protested.

"I *know* it's clean – but I want it *cleaner!*" Mum explained patiently, "*and* I need the top fridge emptied and disinfected. Pine."

"I *hate* that job!" moaned Ophelia.

" That's exactly why I want it doing! Nobody tackles the the top fridge - because it's always full: five hungry mouths to feed... and it's *fiddly*," Mum concurred, "but I *do* go out to work as well!"

In Ophelia's experience, their mother *never* ceased to underline her sacrifice. After all she was one of Leeds City Council's *Empty Retail Premises*' Team: some days able to work from home; more days at the Town Hall : constantly jollying traders to move into, *or back into,* derelict shops.

"And what's *Little Willie* doing?" challenged Candida, deliberately using her younger brother William's shortened name: the one he loathed *anyone* using, most of all his two disrespectful sisters.

"Don't worry! He's sweeping up fallen leaves – and that's a fiddly job as well: because wet, dead leaves keep falling onto growing shrubs.... then onto the *lawn*," Mum pictured.

"Wish he'd do the top fridge as well!"moaned Candida.

"He does what he can!"

"*We'll* believe you!" conceded Candida.

THREE :

It was after Lunch before both girls were back upstairs, having given an already-clean kitchen a lick-&-promise.

Only taking *half* the stuff out of the top fridge: to make it *look* like a supreme effort.

And as a reward for their 'fatigue': at about 12-40 they broken off to eat a good quarter of the available cheese, tomatoes and corned beef they had only just put back to chill! Soon joined by an equally 'starving' William, *also* complaining of exhaustion.

Ensconced in the 'Penthouse' - *how the sisters dubbed the huge roof-space that was their double-bedroom* - Ophelia was busy writing a bit more of her History 'A' level assignment: *'The Six Wives of Henry VIII'* : very pertinent when thinking about the 2 husbands Candida & Ophelia might *-or might not-* acquire a decade later?

"So are we going ahead, *or not* ?" Candida revived their earlier discussion.

"Yes I think so?" replied Ophelia who, in jeans & tee-shirt, suddenly appeared a lot younger than her seventeen-&-a-half.

"When?"

"A week next Friday?" was Ophelia's idea.

14

"Bit soon isn't it?" as not for the first time a note of caution crept into Candida's voice.

"Strike while the iron's hot!"

"I wish you hadn't said that!" Candida referenced in a fit of giggles.
"Sometimes I can't *comprehend* you, Candy: the way your mind works! It's disgusting!" reproved Ophelia.

"Not as bad as yours! Otherwise you wouldn't know along what lines I was thinking!" rejoined Candida.

"Even Willie would know what *you're* thinking. You're always indulging in double meanings!" was Ophelia's subsequent expression of feigned disapproval.

"How about *two* weeks on Friday?" Candida worked out, "That would better accommodate Steve who's coming to tea, a week tomorrow; also Nev who's coming to my Birthday meal the Tuesday after?"

"Smart thinking, Candy! *Other*wise it would arouse all sorts of suspicions." Ophelia could now see the advantages of another 7 days' delay implementing the 'Experiment.' "Two weeks next Friday it is!"

FOUR :

Very soon the two girls would have to decide whether to tell Mum, Dad, William: one of them, two of them, all of them - or none of them?

An obvious place to break news of the swop would be in their weekly Family Conference: usually scheduled for Saturdays, 5-30: an import from Dad's work as a Child Psychologist, his higher degree, elevating him to "Dr. Crabtree," being in Analyses of Human Behaviour.

And all three of this poor Doctor's children *delighted* in saying Dad couldn't be a very good Child Psychologist because he hadn't an imperfect understanding his own kids! Never mind calming longsuffering *Mum* down when she was on the rampage!

Attendance at Family Conference was *not* optional. Dad always insisted it was the glue which held the family together. Each child, in turn, from age of 5 onwards, joined the circle of 5 max where there were 3 *very strict* rules: 1) Nobody was allowed to speak when someone else was speaking : that applying *equally* to Mum & Dad; 2) Nobody was allowed to leave until the very end, except for the loo; & 3) Nobody was to continue

Conference discussion in two's, or three's after Conference ended - except practicalities.

So if any one of the five equal participants had residual anger or resentment - *or strong disagreement* - he or she was to bring this up in Conference itself.

This all worked so well, nine times out of ten, that Ophelia, Candida, & William were baffled why *every* family didn't have one?

Inevitably, odd questions arose between these formal sessions. In which case each child was welcome to seek out their mother who without much hesitation would advise they'd be much better discussing whatever with their father; or seek out father, first, whose considered response was: "Perhaps go and talk to your mother?"

Open goals: as Mum & Dad could be played off against each other! *Except.* Except when in an all-too-rare show-of-force, each parent sussed out what the game was - *and laid down the law.*

One of the obscurities of Crabtree family life was Ophelia and Candida's certainty that *William* was the apple of her parents' eyes: a misperception balanced by *William*'s conviction that *Ophelia* was his mother's favourite, Candida his *father*'s favourite every time, she cosying up to him - or wiggling her bum; *sonny himself* the Outsider.

All good-hearted fun! In reality, there was little hard feeling at the end of the day or end of the week. Outbursts were apologized for. Silences quickly broken. Tears wiped up. Storms quelled.

Even perennial rivals Ophelia & Candida had their own way of being reconciled. Because they *had* to share one bedroom, albeit a big one: a sleeping arrangement they constantly moaned about - so great the need for Mum & Dad to both have little offices of their own ; so opposed their father to either moving from such a lovely Edwardian Semi - *or* to partitioning the girls' 'Penthouse.' Like it or lump it : privacy or *no* privacy.

At the end of each day, Ophelia would lean over to kiss her younger sister on the forehead - or Candida do so in reverse before lights went off; before they both dropped to sleep. In Conference, the warring sisters admitted this was a sometimes resisted means of not letting wounds fester; not letting the sun go down on their anger: anger exaggerated; anger deep-felt, whenever.

FIVE :

At 9 o'clock the following Tuesday evening, Homework completed, more or less, Candida *again* asked Ophelia whether they should tell their mother about the Swop. "No! She might not keep it to herself?" came her older sister's response.

"So what about Dad?" Candida persisted, "it's *his* line of country. He might be quite enthusiastic?"

"Yes: a *real-life* Experiment - like his *interminable* studies of identical twins!" Ophelia enthused, "He could write a Paper for all his peers about *his own* 2 girls breaking new ground: laying themselves on the pyre to prove their devotion to each other - *and* their lovers..."

"I wouldn't get carried away, Phelia!" cried Candida, "it's only for one evening - and only one *segment* of one single evening: hardly *Suttee*! Nor so dire a pyre?"

"But you know what Dad's *like*?" Ophelia argued, "he'd probably kybosh the whole idea! Too risky by half?"

"Yes the only way to play fair is to tell absolutely nobody - not even Little Willie!" Candida agreed.

"Least of all *him!*" Ophelia exclaimed. "He's like a leaking sieve!" Silence.

"But here's hoping secrets is the only thing Willie leaks?"

"Now that really *is* unkind," was Candy's judgment as she leapt to her brother's defence, "*I've* told him things in the past and he's proved a good ally."

"And ev'ryone *knows* you need Allies!" joked Ophelia.

"However..." Candida was about to express some more doubt: "Willie does know Nev quite well...In fact he's been a sort of buddy to Neville longer than me?"

"Even though there's 2 school-years *between* them?" Ophelia checked out.

"Yes they both met in Middle School corridor; both titular fans of *Leeds United*; both know a lot about fish & fishing. Both play darts. And both are into *the Beatles,*" Candida recited, inwardly proud she knew the alliteration 'titular' from *Poetry Platform* each Thursday lunchtime: the same *Platform* that had all its novice poets & poetesses doubled up whenever their

20

facilitator mentioned *'pregnant with joy,'* *'pushing up daisies,'* or *'Joseph not yet knowing Mary.'*

"Yes! They do seem to be a bit close?" Ophelia admitted, "....to the point they probably lend each other records and rods."

"*Two quid* rods!" Candida sneered.

"Two pounds lost - or not?" Ophelia continued, warming to the theme, "I bet Willie's quite chuffed to have a mate going out with his own sister? *I can't think why?* No telling what pleases some folks?" Ophelia taunted: awaiting the response she was absolutely certain her barb would attract:

"Cheeky sod!   Nev's in love with me!"

"In that case either he needs to go to *SpecSavers* - or else he's run out of horses to put his 75p. pocket money on!"

"That's enough!" smarted Candida, with real indignation. "At least he's in a better position than your Steve: *really* running out of talent, having to resort to whatever jumble's left over at the close of a rummage sale!" *That* word-picture restored her so severely-damaged self-esteem.

Leading to her sister's inevitable threat: "You'll *regret* this, Candy! There's *fun* and fun that goes *too far*! And this *was* going too far! We'd best call the whole swop *off*? The whole messy business: *off*. Immediately! You can't be trusted with a kid from Year 7 still sat in his high *chair* ; never mind someone as eminent, as mature, as resourceful, as my Steve!"

"Sorry sis!" Candida whimpered.

SIX :

The William whose discretion had, that evening - unbeknown to himself - been so greatly called into question, was actually remarkably *self-sufficient*. Not the same as self-*satisfied*.

He benefited enormously from a big age gap which wasn't all that big: two-&-a-half years junior to Candida [underline the word *junior*] - four years younger than Ophelia. William often thought that *if* their birth-order had been in *one-year* steps like in some families, the three of them might not have enjoyed such autonomy? Such *relative* independence.

And because William accepted *himself*; moreover, because he was born *male*: he could grow up not *compared* with his sisters; not having to compete with them - except for second-helpings! Above all: allocated a bedroom *of his own.*

Also William was ridiculously healthy: not *quite* a fitness fanatic; but always the lad with the lowest finish-time upon completing fairly gruelling circuit-training in the School gym.

Additionally, William possessed a sense of humour: essential for joshing with Candida, his tease, in particular. Wryly, he told his Year 9 friends how he managed to manage "them two" by winding them up and getting out of the way before the explosion.

Even so, his outward contempt for Candy & Ophelia; and his spurning some of their attentions - including occasionally *unkind* attentions - masked his gratitude - freely expressed - for their *generosity*. Generosity of forgiveness - as well as generosity of Cash.

If ever he needed a pound - *or 50 p.* - to get by, he was sure Phelia or Candy would come up with that sum- and more! Nor would they demand it back within the week. Ophelia even did William's Homework without any of his teachers realizing. In return, climbing *Mount Snowdon*, he'd wait for his sisters to make sure they were keeping up. And with computer games, he'd tell *them* how and when to wield the console.

Candida had not selected *Intermediate Technology* as one of her Year 10 options. So when she - more often than her older sister - got muddled over malware, mouses, menus, sending data, saving data, *retrieving* data, William was on hand to unscramble whatever had been scrambled. And to repay Willie for his patience, the boy always said Candy was a whiz at scrambled egg.

None of these attributes made William a saint. Nor would his sisters necessarily *want* a saint for their sibling. Better their brother knew the boundaries, or at least *some* of them: territory where that rascal should never trespass .

William was never, ever, permitted comment on Ophelia's exotic hair arrangements - though he did! : her buns, beehives, tie-backs, whatever: styles never free of mottled hair-grips, elasticated   bands, or 'curlers.' Nor draw attention to Phelia's renowned collection of rings, bracelets, bangles, pendants or necklaces.

As for the *younger* of his sisters: his mother had warned him never - *for any reason* - to comment on Candida's ample bosom, even when Phelia did. "Candy's just a bit well-developed..." Mum told her only son, as if he had not reached that conclusion already.
And that prohibition still applied when Candy herself chose the tightest of brassieres revealing the lowest of cleavages. Not that Candy's breasts were *enormous.* Nor artificially enhanced: *definitely not.* But those boobs were pronounced enough to leave most of her contemporaries *green* with envy: her teachers doubly cautious.

SEVEN :

The following Saturday morning : exactly one week since Candida & Ophelia had first 'launched' their controversial 'Experiment,' Ophelia actually shifted her position on the swop: "For my part, I'd *certainly* go ahead with our swop. It'll really teach us both something. P'raps a lot? Make Steve appreciate *me* more - and Nev appreciate *you* more?"

"Right-ho!" Candida responded.

"In truth I can't think of two lads *more* attentive to our needs," Ophelia continued, " Nev, in particular, appears to worship the ground you stand on!"

"Indeed!" said Candida. "I know I could do worse. I was once asked out by a boy - then in Year 8 - who smelt of *fish*! And as for the Squaddie Ashley I met at *Roxy's* Disco: he was *creepy*. Bet he was married to some woman back in barracks! He kept saying I was the loveliest girl he'd ever seen. Did I want to watch him in the Drill Hall? Pulling a Bus with a rope! Well, he was at least 4 years older than me, possibly five..?"

"Therein lies the difficulty , Candy. Because Steve will be about six years older than you!" Ophelia reminded her sister.

"But he's not of the same rank as Private Ashley!" Candida suggested, "We've got something of *a flavour* of Steve - *and you've road-tested him!*"

"Thankyou very much!" Here Ophelia's voice was tinged with exasperation: "Steve's not an old banger I'm buying second-hand from a dodgy dealer!"

"But he *might* be second-hand?" Candida contended: curious to see how her sister dealt with that possibility.

"Well I think he's so *caught up* with his work-life, girlfriends don't come to him naturally?"

"Till *you* came along!" Candida chuckled, "to show him what he was missing?"
"Well I wasn't an *ad*junct, if that's what you mean? Nor a trophy for him to bring out on special occasions?" Ophelia pointed out.

To which Candida was at her most provocative: "Until he *unwrapped* his trophy?"

"Candy: you really *are* very rude - and you seem to *enjoy* being crude!" Now it was Ophelia only *pretending* to be shocked: "If - and it's *a big If* - we ever do go ahead with this arrangement, I know for sure that you'll dig and dig deep into my - *I mean our* - relationship till you've either wrecked it - or learnt something unflattering about *me*?"

"But what's the point of spending 4 or 5 hours in the company of an *old* - I mean older - man when I can see what's unflattering about you by sticking right here *where I am*?" asked Candida, fully expecting the swipe over the head with a pillow which her older sister duly delivered.

"And while we're on the subject of impersonators, you never know, Candy, what *I* shall discover when I get your Nev on his own and catch *him* off-guard?" Ophelia sent an imaginary tennis ball screaming across an imaginary net to land in Candida's court on the opposite side of the loft.

"Well *I've* got nothing to worry about, Phelia!" boasted the younger sister, "What you'll see in Nev is what you'll get: the heart Amanda never reached?"

That touching image really impressed Ophelia. Because she now knew - *if she did not understand it before* - that, despite Candy's immaturity - Neville's immaturity too?- her sister was laying out her stall for anybody & everybody to see: even awarding bitter love-rival Mandy her full name.

"In that case I'll wait *and see!*" Ophelia concluded triumphantly.

EIGHT :

For two hours before their Saturday Lunch, both girls cleaned the inside of every window in *Clovelly* : Ophelia in her mother's Study trying to resist the temptation to read whatever had been left on her desk; Candida in her *father*'s Study trying to resist the temptation to read any notes left out on *his* desk.

"What's the point of cleaning the *insides* of all these windows?" Candida never failed to ask Mum - whenever the *'Rota of Chores'* required it. No need to clean *inside* when the official window-cleaner was employed to do the *out*side?

Meanwhile, it was *William*'s job, that day, to do the fridge & freezer. No harsh ice-scrapers for him. Instead he carefully placed saucepans of boiling water on each of the freezer's four shelves to melt the accumulated ice which then peeled off in the sort of chunk that could easily be thrown out of the back door.

After all their exertions, the three young people sat down to a well-deserved snack Lunch : in turn releasing William from the constraints of Family Conference. Freeing him to make acerbic comments regarding his sisters' Suitors. *And Willie wasn't going to waste the opportunity.*

Both girls earnestly attempted to shut their ears to all Willie's largely untrue - and definitely unsolicited - Peer Review. And, needless to say, when their brother *realized* how discomfiting was his running commentary: the funnier that commentary became.

Having said that, William would never *knowingly* torpedo his sisters' love affairs. In fact he *had* been known so to praise the young man concerned; to make his feedback so saccharine, that Candy or Phelia smelt a rat and switched to somebody else. Mission accomplished!

In *Clovelly,* William had his own territory, physically and emotionally: quite cut off at the end of the first-floor corridor. Nobody really bothered if he broadcast loud music: rap, pop, hip-hop, rap, garage, whatever; provided no sound of any sort came out of his room after 9-30 pm. And although Willie *did* have access to an old-fashioned 1911 wash-basin in his bedroom - '*H&C*' as Seaside Boarding Houses used always to call it: Candy & Phelia teased him he hadn't yet cottoned on to what that wash-stand was *for?*

NINE :

When the two girls next talked about the swop - *something of an obsession of late* - Candida quipped: "Must get you enrolled for M-eye-six Ophelia!" *Not* the end of her irreverence. "Actually it might still be a good idea not to tell Willie *or* Mum *or* Dad, definitely *not* tell Steve or Nev."

"And we'll both stick to a Friday," Ophelia continued, "even though we'll both have to avoid each other! Friday's our *usual* day for dating - or, if there is no date, for hanging out with the Year. We mustn't change night - or we'll be *rumbled*."

Candida concurred: " *Yes* : Carole and Nicky, Jayne & Jasmine are amazed how we manage to adhere to the 'Friday-night rule.' Monday to Thursdays: homework; Saturdays & Sundays for family. Most of them go out *any* evening of the week - with very few questions *asked*."

"Unlike for us two! It's like the Spanish Inquisition. <<Where have you gone?>>; <<What have you drunk?>> ; <<Who's seeing you home?>> ; <<How do we know you've gone where you say you've gone?>>." Ophelia's rattled through Mum's frequently-asked questions, each time imitating her mother's solicitous voice. Enquiries entirely immediately familiar to her younger sister: <<Take care!>> ; <<You know what boys are like!>> ; <<Ring us to let us know you've safely arrived...>> ; <<Remember long waits for a Bus!>>

"Don't talk about it! *Too much*! Much too much! We're being *tracked*! We're being *stalked*!" Candida's voice rose in mock complaint.

"Police state! - but I'd *still* rather that than being allowed to go anywhere at any time..." Ophelia conceded.

"Do you remember when you were grounded for 7 whole days, Candy?" the older sister continued: "for being an hour-&-a-half late back from School *without letting anyone know*?"

"Better than *you*, Phelia!" Candida recalled: "grounded for 14 whole days for filling your refillable water bottle with white wine from the fridge, claiming it was cheapo apple-juice? Fancy that!"

"Well I *did* fancy that. The two *do* look exactly the same. And you would have done exactly the same! My sin was *being found out*!"

At this point, Ophelia went off to the *en suite* to fill up their private electric kettle ready for some more coffee.

TEN :

"Bet they never cross-question Willie? *A boy!*" Candida alleged, half-an-hour later, when their deliberations re-commenced.

"*Oh yes they do!*" Ophelia contradicted. "In fact they're harder on him than on us - lest they're awarded a premature grandchild! A Moses-in-the-Basket hidden among the bull-rushes. Lest he's caught with his ...."

Candida didn't wait to curtail her Sister's speculation as to the ankles where their brother's chinos might land : "I *think* you mean a baby premature *in timing*? Not, Heaven Forbid, born at 30 weeks?"

Silence.

"*Anyway,*" Candy continued: "I'm sure our Willie wouldn't know what to do! He'd be tempted to clear out of his once-a-year PSE Sex Lesson. He'd think his prime visual aid - a banana - was there to *eat* : rather than to be clothed in accordance with his very indulgent School Nurse's instructions?"

At this observation, Ophelia creased up with laughter. Between her giggles she spluttered: "*Candy*: I think it's *me* who would eat the banana. I've always been rather partial to them. And before you insinuate....."

Now it was *Candida*'s turn to be convulsed: "*Stop it! Stop it!*"

Yet just a few minutes later, Ophelia returned to the subject: "Well *someone*'s got to show him the ropes!"

"And it certainly won't be his Dad?" finished off Candida: "Because he'd have to tell his son the means by which Willie came into the world, courtesy willy."

"And I thought *I* was the *only* awful girl round here, me being more *experienced*!" concluded Ophelia triumphantly.

"I like the way you trumpet your *experience*." objected Candida: "as if you're some *femme fatale*. As if you're the 6th-Form scrubber, bathed in red light and all that?"

"That's because, *unlike you*, I don't *need* red backlights to draw lads to me like the Queen Bee..." boasted Ophelia with mock-cruelty.

ELEVEN

Sunday Number 2 was odd : both a help and a hindrance in establishing - *and getting away with* - the forthcoming Swop.

Occasionally Mum invited the latest Flame - if there was one - always provided he or she looked like *a serious proposition* - to Tea: knowing full well that Tea with the Crabtrees would be quite enough to extinguish most Flames. *On the spot!*

Sunday Tea was supposed to be a formal - but not an intimidating - occasion : a chance for all three children, plus boyfriend - or one of the girls' girlfriends - to shine. This meal much less structured than *Saturday*'s Family Conference: that a slot so immovable it was convened *even when the family was away on holiday*.

"Why not show Stephen off to the rest of the family?" Mum had beamed - *without* going one step further and highlighting how the Crabtrees would also be on show *to Steve*. Was this perhaps *an examination*? - Candida often asked herself: a test most teenagers - certainly most amorous *squaddies* - would inevitably *fail*.

In turn, each guest was told *not* to bring a gift. *Nor a bouquet.* Just bring themselves.

Sunday September 29th. was, coincidentally in the light of the girls' intense debates of late: *Ophelia's* turn to invite whoever: in this case her boyfriend - *or man-friend* - of 4 months' standing. Ever since she first encountered him at a Year 12 Careers' Convention.

This was also his first time over the doorstep: arousing *more* curiosity because, at 22-ish, Steve was considerably older than *any* of Ophelia's previous boyfriends: "old enough to be Phelia's father," as Candy had observed - with quite a margin of inaccuracy.

Other families might have found this Sunday ritual stupid: far too fancy, far too overblown. Equally most families would resist a weekly Family Conference - indeed, *any Family Conference whatsoever.* On the ground that if you don't dig too deep you won't come up with any buckets of coal.

Guest Teas, however, came into Eleanor Crabtree's category of " *If they don't like it, they can lump it.*"

After all, this was her Psychologist husband's *home turf.*

Applied Psychology. Anybody *not* welcoming the Invite could turn the Invitation down!

Nor would turning down a Crabtree Invitation diminish Wiliam, or Candida, *or* Ophelia's, friendliness towards their friends - *nor* were any of them angling for a *return* Invite. They realised some students -*indeed many adults*- suffer from social phobia; in the extreme, *agoraphobia* - through no fault of their own. Accepting Mrs. Crabtree's invitation was a *two-way* acceptance - acceptability too? If anyone *was* inclined to accept - which Steve evidently *was*!

Steve's alacrity to accept threw the object of his affections, Ophelia, into a tizwoz. Would Willie or Candy - *or Mum*- drop a clanger? Also, could *Dad* keep his conversation sufficiently bland? Stripped of controversy? *Ophelia herself* might be shown up in less favourable light? Dad   recalling embarrassing incidents from her *pre*-adolescence? Even the dreaded *Photo Album* might make an appearance?

TWELVE :

Steve actually arrived a quarter-of-an-hour *before* the stated time of 4-45.

Did he reason arriving early is infinitely more polite than being late?

And it was *Candida* who chanced to open the door. She had not met Steve before - but had seen 4 or 5 photos. And seemed determined to add to her overall picture of him this evening.

So there she was in the doorway in neat rouged pink top, demure pillar-box red skirt , divided by a 5"-deep, patent black belt.

"You'd better come in," she muttered, as if the person on their doorstep was the Insurance Man.

"I thought that was the idea," quipped Steve.

Candida then asked *"May I take your coat & scarf?"*- just as she might were she the P.A. welcoming a Solicitor's newest client.

"So you're Ophelia's *sister*?" the visitor asked.

"I presume so!" confirmed Candida, "Glad you can join our picnic on the back lawn!"

But before she could wind the poor man up further, Ophelia - attired in simple navy-blue dress - appeared from further down the corridor. "Don't listen to her, Steve!" she chided, "we *do* like eating outdoors-caravanning and all that - but today we're *in*side."

"*Good*!" Steve responded, "Otherwise I'd better take that coat back again? Then - because Candida hadn't *yet* disappeared - he added: "You told me you had *one* other sister? Now I've met her, I understand!"

Cue for younger sister to flirt: "Phelia's jolly lucky to have a sister like me! I'm the meet-er and greet-er round here!" Candida always liked the way these two words rhymed. *Might she have first heard them in Leeds/Bradford Airport Arrivals?*

At that precise moment, Mum appeared : " *Hello Stephen*! Is it all right if I also call you *Steve*? We're *very* informal!"

"Indeed, Mrs. Crabtree! Your daughter has been looking after me *very well*," was his fulsome compliment as he turned round, again, to face Candida.

"And young William can't *wait* to meet you as well!" she bubbled, prompting Steve's effort at a joke: "Pardon me! I thought it was *Phelia* who couldn't wait to see me?"

"Yes, my sister's been like a cat-on-hot-tiles waiting for you! She's wanted to try her perm, also her new tone of lipstick, for ages!" Here Candida exploited to the full that she was still guarding the closed front door, not Steve's *intended* partner.

"Don't listen to this *tiresome* child !" Ophelia scolded, "Pity *me* who has to live with her *all the time*!"

"I won't — if you say so Madam?" Steve groaned, as he obediently followed the 2 girls into the Lounge.

THIRTEEN :

Round the tea table at 5-15, it was *Dad* who opened conversation : "I hear you're in *shipping*, Stephen?" Here he sounded just like the President of *Beeston Rotary Club* welcoming its newest member.

Before Steve had chance to reply, *William* piped up: "Yes, he *rows*! Hires a rowing-boat at the little wooden hut at *King George VI* Park!"

From anyone else's lips but Willie's this would have been a diplomatic disaster. Instead, everyone was laughing.

"You're an *awful*, boy ! Don't *any*one listen to him!" growled Ophelia.

"Yes I insure vessels against the possibility of their sinking - or another catastrophe such as loss of cargo."

Before Steve could elaborate further, Dad continued his line of questioning: "So you have to balance out all the risks? Must require a good grasp of maritime law?"

"Yes. Several ships aren't insurable: flying under all sorts of dubious flags."

And that led Dr. Crabtree to add gravely: "There *might* even be some reappearance of a phenomenon we all thought was anchored in the *past* : Piracy."

"*Piracy!* " Candida whispered, seeming to enjoy hearing a word from her childhood.

Cue for William - deciding, for once, to be serious - to chime in: "Well I, for one, don't think Pirates are very *funny*!"

"Well done, William!" his Dad responded: " I'm glad you've been able to see *behind* all those polka-dotted masks, three-pointed caps, skulls-&-crossbones!" -

41

before crowning his stricture with the verdict: " *I* don't find murder on the high seas at all funny *either*!"

"*Murder on the High Seas!*" echoed Candida, "sounds like an ITV Drama! Mutiny ... and walking *the plank*!"

"Well I think we should *stop* talking about Shipping - and start *eating*!" a hitherto dumbstruck Eleanor Crabtree urged, "Steve's here for *Salad* Days: not a Busman's Holiday!"

"And *what* a Salad your Phelia has dressed for you!" Candida beamed, "just help yourself!"

"I don't know where to start!" admitted their Guest, "this is the sort of Salad they'd lay out in So*rrent*o: sun-dried tomatoes, green peppers, yellow peppers, stuffed olives, 5-beans, balls of brie, hard-boiled eggs! Where do I *start*?"

"Start anywhere!" exclaimed Mum - "and, on the trencher, there's ham, tongue & *Melton Mowbray* Pork Pie..."

"Yes I cycled all the way to Melton Mowbray to fetch it!" William quipped, "returning via Stilton for the cheese!"

"*Silly boy!* Don't listen to him, Steve!" admonished an increasingly irritated Ophelia.

"He means well, Sis!" interjected Candida, "Willie's merely stressing how your friend is *worth* all the effort."

Conversation then turned to Leeds as a City: England's second - or third? - City and its Cultural & Retail Offering for the 21st. Century.

FOURTEEN

And when Steve was half-way through his modest plateful of lettuce, pickled onions, coleslaw, cold chipolatas, whatever: half standing-up, he asked Ophelia's mother: "Will you excuse me? All this wonderful spread. *May I use your toilet?*"

"Indeed! The Guest Toilet is immediately opposite you at the top of the stairs," Mrs. Crabtree directed.

"You certainly won't wander into Willie's room *by mistake!*" Candida helpfully added, "*his* door has got an enormous road-sign on it : 'NO ENTRY'!"

"Thankyou!   I'll make sure not to break that prohibition," Steve promised - as an oblique grin broke over said William's face.

" *Do you think we've over-faced him?*" queried Candida.

" No!" Ophelia speedily explained, "Steve's always had a digestion issue. IBS he calls it..."

" Sounds like that disease cattle get: BSE, *Scrapie?* We learnt all about it in...." began an unrepentant William.
"Shut *up!*" Ophelia shrieked, "we're in the middle of eating - and we don't want any Warnings issued by the Ministry of Agriculture!"

"Certainly *not!*" her Mother concurred," there's a time & place for everything - and this is *not* the right time *or place* to discuss a Guest's inner workings."

"Or hers!" muttered a faintly-amused Candida, before receiving a kick from under the table.

"Ouch!"

ΩΨΩΨΩΨΩΨΩΨΩ

FIFTEEN

Upon their Guest's re-appearance, Candida, *pretending* to be relaxed , asked Steve to share which School he went to in an earlier life.

"*St. Cuthbert's*.... a very fine place to learn ." answered Stephen, unawares.

"But that's *private* !" gasped Dad in astonishment.

"Of course it's *private* ! It's run by *monks*," chipped in Ophelia, defensively, " but Boarders can come from any religion!"

"But monks and nuns are permitted to teach in *State* schools!" Dad spluttered.

"Perhaps not if they come from a closed order?"   a slightly shocked Stephen replied.

"They've made a vow of silence," was William's intelligent contribution: "so they're not much good Teaching kids like *us*!"

Perhaps seeing problems ahead , Eleanor, ever tactful, announced: " Well I don't think a little boy is given any *choice* which school he goes to: public or private. If Stephen's Pop wanted *St. Cuthbert's*, then *St. Cuthbert's* it had to be."

"*But*, but..." intercepted Dr. Donald, putting down his buttered scone in some haste.

It was now *Candida's* turn to make everybody sit back & enjoy their Tea: " Well, *I* wasn't asked which school *I* wanted to go to. I think I would have been happier studying in the *countryside*. A *Forest* School? *That's* where I would have got a great deal further than cramming for my GCSEs at *Alderman Cornfield's*."

"Now *outdoors* is where you would have learnt about the birds and the bees!" Ophelia added.

Everyone hooted at that; and the talk went on to whether Stephen had any brothers or sisters.

"No."

"Do you live in a rented flat?"

"No... I *own* it... or soon *shall* own it."

"This isn't a *benefits'* review!" objected Ophelia, "he's not started his Victoria Sandwich yet!"

"*Let them eat cake!*" quoted Candida - to more howls of laughter.

"Not if Ophelia's baked it!" William added as a qualifier.

At that, his mother put on her apron of mock sternness : "*William!* You risk being sent to your bedroom on bread-&-water!   Be much *kinder* to your Sister. *I'm* looking *forward* to Ophelia's Victoria Sponge - which always has a lightness that eludes my efforts."

"*Oh so true!*" smirked Candida - whilst their V.I.P. Guest very wisely held his counsel; instead turning his attention to cutting *his* wedge of said sponge into 4 more-or-less equal segments.

"Stephen! I want you to know that *if* your first impression of *Clovelly* is entering a Madhouse?" father paused for breath, "that's *not* Ophelia's fault. A Child Psychologist's house could never function without a degree of imbecility. *That's what we do!*"

"Speak for *yourself* Donald!" chided Eleanor Crabtree, correcting her husband: " it's a *myth* about doctors unable to heal themselves - or *cobblers* who allow their own children to go unshod..."

"Well *I'm* unshod!" protested Candida. "When I begged for a pair of *Doc Marten's* I was told save up for them myself - *and I can't!*"

"Boo-hoo!" feigned a far-from-sympathetic William.

"*Please* excuse this lot, Steve!" Ophelia begged.

"I will! Truly *I will!* Coming here gives me a different *perspective.*"

Gratified by Stephen's tolerance, Eleanor continued: "There's always a seat reserved for you at *Clovelly*! I think I can understand what led our Ophelia in your direction *If only for all the Lifts you give her?*"

SIXTEEN :

As Steve put on his coat and made for the front door, he beamed so radiantly at Ophelia that she gave him rather a perfunctory farewell:

"Steve: *thanks* for coming! I hope your appetite is sated. Even if it was my cake?"

"A *perfect* cake if I might say it... *first of many more to come?*"

"Nice to meet you, Steve!" chimed in Candida, "you certainly experienced us *as we are! Crazy!*"

Doubtless flashing through Ophelia's mind was slight regret at the prospect of herself assenting to Candida having a whole evening with *her* boyfriend . Would her younger sister take advantage? *Or he*? Surely *not*.

Reappearing out of the Lounge, her father banished many of her doubts: Stephen having safely driven off a few moments earlier: "I think you've chosen *well*! Stephen appears to be very polite – very responsible: even if he did go to *St. Cuthbert's*. But watch out! He's much *older* than you. You've got to make sure he hasn't got a *past*!"

Ophelia didn't know how to take this latter warning - except it didn't sound like something she herself would have said? "We *all* have a past, Dad !.... and I *do know* all about cradle-snatchers: older men trying to get off with younger girls. But Steve isn't *one of them*. He's just been a little wrapped up with his job... *till he met me!*"

Candida was still only on Step Four of going upstairs - &
hanging on to every word.

"Till he met *me!*" she crowed in repetition. "His heart's
desire! His other end of the rainbow! .... Dad's right: get
a life *history* from him. Maybe he's also dating an
Underwriter in London: *someone he met at HQ?*"

Realizing a fight was about to begin, Dad attempted to
stamp on the embers: "Stephen's possibly all he
acknowledges himself to be. I *know* you're sensible,
Ophelia. You were even a dutiful friend whilst *Callum*
was on the scene: a fine *outdoors'* sort of chap. Fresh
air! Lots of hiking!" Dad then paused in case he had said
too much: "You're sensible!   Often too sensible!
Mother & I just don't want you to get hurt..."

Ophelia was fully familiar with the *'Mum & I'* device:
"Well I'll go and tell her, too, that I'm *perfectly* capable
of sticking up for myself! I *do* know how to separate the
wheat from the chaff."

"Chaff!" parroted Candida, provocatively. Ophelia's
younger Sister had *still* only reached Stair number Eight.

"Ignore her, Dad!"

"That I will attempt to do! I can see how splendidly you're operating as Deputy Head Girl - and how well you relate to your mother who must have been seventeen-&-a-half once-upon-a-time?"

"I'm afraid I don't always manage Mum as well as I ought!" grinned Ophelia, "any more than you do! Mum's a *stickler*!"

"As *you* are, my dear! Demanding of yourself the very best."

"Thankyou, Dad!" – Ophelia responded as she hugged him tight.

_____

SEVENTEEN

Although Candida was fairly pleased with her standing following her first opportunity to inspect Steve - a standing she always compared and contrasted with her sister's - she was too weary to work out all the implications of a swop - *the* swop - till after turning the lights off at night two days later.

By then, 10 days after their initial discussions, Candida was getting a little nervous – tinged with excitement that she could - & surely would - outdo her sister in enjoying an older man's attention. Each boy who'd asked her out in the past 18 months: the age a boy might reasonably expect her to split from the comforting hunting-pack of giggly girls, had been a bit immature, unkempt even: the sort of lad she might josh with at the outdoor Lido, but that would be it.

Neville whom she was now *almost ready* to share with her older sister, *for one night only*, was a different kettle of fish from his class-mates: more private, less brash: mysterious enough for her to want to get to know him- in fierce competition from Mandy Tinkerton whom she surmised had wrapped her tentacles right round him.

But what if their plan was botched? Worse: *discovered*? What if the Swop *itself* crash-landed? Perhaps she herself would not be in the right mood, a week on Friday, to meet Steve? He might then take the huff and drive straight to *Clovelly* to see where Ophelia was? Which would inescapably put her parents in the embarrassing position of joining a plot whose execution they might have already designated a lost cause?

And what if poor Nev saw her older sister heading towards him and turn *about-heels* in order to reach the sanctuary of his home porch before risking damaging his burgeoning friendship with *herself*?

It was vital Steve *didn't* see Ophelia on the night itself - *or* Neville see Candida. Whatever paths might on another night converge or overlap must be kept miles apart. *Miles.*

Mandy Tinkerton was still rather sweet on Nev: her need to get him back proportionate to her fervent desire to banish Candida to the sidelines forever. But it was *she* who'd dumped Nev for two weeks of fun with the notoriously unreliable Carl Simmons of Lower Sixth.

It struck Candida as her mind raced ahead in bed that Tuesday - too much black coffee? - that Nev had never gone into much detail regarding Amanda. It could have been an innocent crush, but - without Carl Simmons' sweet nothings to come - would surely have gone somewhere? If only to spite Candy who'd established herself on the under-17s' hockey-field as Centre-Half: a position Mandy had always considered *her own by merit*. Nor, earlier this year, had Mandy won the Year 10 Poetry Prize to follow successive successes in 2000 and 2001, Candida herself coming *second* in 2001.

And - as if their rivalry was not already intense enough- Candy had boobs fully-developed - maybe *too* fully? - set against a still-pretty Mandy's still to show.

So, as Candida drifted into delayed slumber, she told herself there was still much work to do preparing the ground for the Big Experiment, avoiding any pratfalls along the way.

EIGHTEEN

On the Wednesday nine days in advance of the Swop, both Sisters realised they needed first to discuss *practicalities*; second, ways to safeguard all 4 people involved from having cats let out of the bag.

"The only way our swop will work is if we've got plausible excuses not to be with the two people we're supposed to be with," said Ophelia.

" Yes we've got to be ill !" agreed Candida, "Very ill! .. or perhaps *not*?" A note of doubt entered her voice as she glanced down at her developing - developing too quickly? - body, without it showing any signs of malaise.

"Yes: the trick is to be *ill* - but not *gravely* ill... or else Steve & Nev will likely report back to Mum & Dad - worse to Steve's own parents - *and* to Neville's Marilyn?" the older sister reasoned.

"So how are we going to avoid storing up all sorts of problems? How are we going to tell *white* lies without fibbing big-way: covering up mild untruths with great big whoppers?" Candida kept up the questioning.

"True! I can just imagine Steve ditching you, Candy, and heading straight for *Emergency Ward 10* to ascertain whether I'm on life-support!" This scenario obviously troubled Ophelia.

"That brings us straight back to *timing*. Our respective meetings must be at *exactly* the same time - preferably miles away from each other." Here Candida's cool logic came into play.

"Yes our illnesses, *our indispositions*, must be mild enough to keep the paramedics out; also to stop Mum calling an Ambulance for fear of Meningitis!" Ophelia worried.

"Yes: ever since Dawn in Lower Sixth contracted Meningitis and was 4 weeks knocking at death's door,

Mum's been petrified of undiagnosed Sepsis," Candida acknowledged.

"So <<a bit off colour>> is what it is: what women have always called <<a bad headache.>>" Ophelia concurred.

"Yes, let's play *the time-of-month* card!" Candida reaffirmed. "Steve will swallow that whole, because he *always* meets up with you on <<the wrong day of the month >>!"

"That's not very funny, Candy! In fact Menstruation's no subject for mirth," Ophelia responded indignantly. "It's *you* who scares Nev - or whoever - to the core: with *your* moodiness!"

NINETEEN

An hour later, the girls' discussion turned to what to tell their Mother: " Yes: we'll *have* to get it get past Mum." Ophelia concluded, " we've got to let her in on the act!"

Candida was however far less certain: "We can't!" she exclaimed. " Mum'ud squash the whole idea - or at least pour cold water on our swop."

"We can - *and we must* - tell her!" the older girl insisted. "Then in her own good time *she'll* tell Dad. That makes Mum our *shield* if anything goes wrong."

"But please leave William out of the curve!" Candy pleaded.

"*Conceded!* Tipping off William *would* be a step too far! But *after* it's all over he'll see the joke," Ophelia predicted.

"Do you think Mum'll *allow* us to fib ?" asked Candida.

"Its not really a matter of *fibbing*," Ophelia conjectured, " because *all* girls have periods."

"But all girls *don't* go out and make merry while they've got their period pains !" Candida added with doubt in her voice.

"I still think Mum'll agree provided we 're upfront *why* we're doing it. Testing feelings: mine to Steve; Steve to me; yours to Nev; Nev's to you," reasoned Ophelia.

"And we'll only develop women's problems *late* that Friday." Candida sounded relieved.

"Very late –*far* too late for us to text either boy... I mean 'man' in Steve's case."   Ophelia now sounded more confident too.

"That makes it sound *very* exciting : doing it.... I mean not doing it, standing them up," giggled Candida.

"But we're *not* standing them up," continued the older sister: "in fact, standing somebody up, risking a wild goose-chase: that's very rude. Only a last resort... when 2 lovers have really fallen *out of* love with each other, and want to make a point. Otherwise, it's *wrong!*"
"Yes the beauty of our arrangement next week is that both chaps will be surprised & delighted!" Here, unconsciously, Candida was copying Royalty, how they always gave out their news.

"*Or not*? Surprised - but *not* delighted!" Ophelia wanted to introduce a final note of hesitancy - because she still thought of herself as 'cradle-snatcher' : one of her reference points: Actress Barbara Windsor.

ΩΨΩΨΩΨΩΨΩΨΩ

TWENTY

That *Thursday* evening, after Lessons followed by 6th-Form *Dancing Society*, a rather sweating Ophelia buttonholed her mother in her office: " I want to bounce an idea off you." she started.

"That normally means you've made up your mind already ! " Eleanor chuckled... Sit down anyway!"

"I'm here on Candy's behalf as well."

"Good heavens! You must be speaking to each other!"

"We're not that bad! – at least not *today,*" Ophelia gulped. "We want to swop boyfriends next Friday night: to breathe a bit of fresh air in, if you see what I'm saying..."

"Stop there!" Mum interrupted: " Have you fallen *out* with Steve - or Candida had a duff text from Neville?

"No! Definitely not I The opposite, in fact... as you & Dad saw last Sunday Tea. We just want to see how each of them behaves in the company of somebody else. Outside their comfort zone..."

"And then you'll both be jealous of everything you hear about how the other person's night has gone!" opined Ophelia's mother :"Surely a recipe for disaster if ever there was one!"

"No we've thought it through: through and through - and that's why the two of us are seeking your blessing on the adventure."

"Venture you mean? Or possibly you *do* mean Adventure," replied Mum, now firmly wearing her 'Wife-of-Psychologist' hat. " Well the whole idea still sounds ridiculous! There'll be bucket-loads of tears ... Also it could throw both courtships out of kilter?"

"They're not courtships!" sparked up Ophelia, decisively. "Courtship's something you do when you're going steady; when you're saving up hard; when you're thinking of having a baby!"

At this forecast of her girls' future Mum gasped with a mixture of horror & incredulity. But kept silent.

"You see? We just wanna have fun!" announced elder daughter, devotedly quoting *the Spice Girls*.

"So are you saying that playing with 2 boys' emotions; tossing those emotions high in the air to see where they'll land; monumentally *confusing* each lad -*and each other*- is FUN?" Eleanor Crabtree hissed, perhaps rhetorically.

"We'd certainly not set out to *upset* anybody, at least not intentionally, Mum! And we're both fully up-to-speed on knowing what we're entering into..."

"This business of 'entering into' comes from the *Book of Common Prayer* - and sounds far more complicated than exchanging boyfriends for one night!" Mum gathered, blissfully unaware her Ophelia thought 'entering into' came from the *Karma Sutra*.

"True we've thought about the scheme *and* talked about it *and* drawn the conclusion it would give both of our friendships, maybe our *future* friendships, a fillip"

Before Ophelia had greater opportunity to justify the Experiment - and before she could congratulate herself for re-discovering the word 'fillip' which sounded so similar to Philip Glass the 6th.former who had wanted to be voted Head Boy this year - her mother began her summing up: " Scheme? You're too *right*, Ophelia, to call it a 'scheme.' A far nicer word, if I might say so, than *Scam*? The notion of a simple swop is silly - also incredibly short-sighted; but it *is* novel - and you both deserve credit for wanting to breathe new life into any close relationship you have, or might have, or might - *or might not* - be prepared to throw overboard."

"Just like the sort you and Dad reinvented?"

"*Enough* of that young lady!" intercepted mother with mock indignation: "Try it out! But don't *either* of you dare to come back to me in a fortnight's time in floods of tears: begging my sympathy that you got it all wrong!"

"We won't, Mum! And thanks for *listening*!" at which point Ophelia got up and made haste back upstairs to tell Candy the good news.

TWENTY-ONE

"Glad that's over!" Ophelia sighed as she sat on the end of her sister's bed. "Went far better than either of us could have thought it would. And it's a weight off my shoulder knowing Mum's been let in on our secret."

"*Yes*, secrets are very hard to keep in a close-knit family.." began Candida as Ophelia grunted at the very notion they were consistently - or ever? - *close-knit*.

"At least Mum's now on board," Ophelia smiled, "I don't really mean *fully on board*. She thinks we'll both sink! But at least she hasn't ordered us to call it all off!"

"In fairness, Mum's not usually the ordering *sort.* She prefers to steer her ship between jagged rocks using a tiller..." Here Candida found what she thought was the right metaphor.

"Very clever!" replied her older Sister with a spoonful of sarcasm. "Mum's certainly been primed to keep us all on course - without us knowing we're *being* steered!"

"Now we just need to plan who'll be there, where and when, a week on Friday - without anyone knowing any better?" Candida amplified.

"So we'd better begin practising being *unwell!*" suggested Ophelia, "Gotta look the part: fairly down-in-the-dumps - but not clapped-out sufficiently to turn up in the wrong place at the wrong time - rather *well enough* to turn up still in the wrong place but, this time, at the right time!"

"The trouble is: I *do* feel well!" interjected Candida. "That's why I've hardly ever been able to throw a sickie to get out of School! Dad *always* rumbles me!"

"Too true!" Ophelia agreed. "Although Dad's a doctor of the mind, *and mental*, he seems to know enough about coughs & colds, aches & pains, severely damaged vertebrae, disjointed elbows, whatever, to suss us out and send us off to School regardless!"

"Yes we could be *half-dead*!" shrieked Candida: "and we'd *still* have to go to School. Dad'ud even tear up our sick-notes is he thought we'd forged them!"

"Bet there's nobody who hasn't written their own sick-note!" proffered Ophelia, " Cept everyone else will get away with it, at least twice a year..."

"While there's an orgy taking place is some kid's flat : both parents out at work?" lamented Candida, " an orgy you can only go to if you're off School *sick*!"

"Wish I knew as much about orgies as *you* do, Sis!" pondered Ophelia, "the only Party *I* got to when I was in Year 10 or 11 was a *Methodist Youth Club* Squash, playing 'Charades' and 'Pass-the-Parcel': hardly the work of the Devil!"

"Yes I don't think either of us would be everso comfortable in a *real* orgy - but it does sound a lot more exciting than Girl Guides singing '*Nymphs & Shepherds*' round a camp-fire!" recollected Candida looking down to her blouse as if to identify her nine sewn-on badges."

"Depends what those nymphs & shepherds are getting up to?" Ophelia wondered.

"Just like *you,* Phelia: you read lots into *any* Song when you try - even '*Men of Harlech.*' ! "

At that journey of the imagination into their belovèd North Wales, Candida went to the toilet, then tried to bury herself in Commerce homework.

_____

TWENTY-TWO

When Eleanor Crabtree got the opportunity to tell Dr. Donald, the girls' father, about their novel plan, she chose an evening when she might get his *full* attention: the Friday seven days before the Friday of the Experiment: both girls out with other girls from School that evening.

"A swop is what they want - or don't want, whichever way round you put it."

"A swop of Boyfriend, *surely not?*" Dad queried.

"Yes: a fair exchange - but *for one night only...*"

"One night only? I'm sorry I just don't see the point?" Donald Crabtree sounded puzzled. "Trying something different: I mean trying some-*one* different, for *a single evening* won't tell them anything - except confusing everybody involved."

"True, it *is* silly!" Eleanor admitted. " True it *is* hair-brained. But the two of them seem to have talked it through and seem to have weighed up the advantages."

"Advantages? " Donald now sounded even *more* sceptical: "I can only see advantage, *obscure* advantage, if all four of them going out *together* on a jolly: that a far better arena to clarify how each girl feels about each boy; each boy about each girl."

"Well I think Phelia & Candy are of an age when they don't want to get *too* serious. When they want to try out more transient relationships," the girls' mother reasoned.

"Who knows, Eleanor? Phelia, for instance, might need more persuading about Stephen? She might be searching for *verification*," argued Dr. Donald.

"Verification! That sounds awfully like the word 'Valuation': as in 'Self-Valuation' - or 'Validation': in the sense of 'Self-Validation' : which you keep bringing up in Family Conference till everybody *groans!*" recollected her children's mother, with a mixture of impatience and tease in her voice.

"Never be a Psychologist in *one's own* household!" her husband then maintained - as he never failed to remind everyone who would listen.

"Well if you tried to psychologise *me*- except in jest - you'd be summoned to Divorce Court in a trice!" Eleanor threatened without her husband-of-22-years *looking* threatened.

"So is it our duty, Eleanor, to *forbid* the swop?" At this moment, Doctor Donald didn't sound at all certain of his own prescription.

"Definitely not!" his wife interjected: hesitant no longer. "They're young *and strong*, and not likely to warm to edicts: merely seeking occasional *advice*..."

"Well those two little Madams don't come and seek *my* advice!" grumbled Donald.

"Come off it!" Eleanor responded straightway. "Candy, in particular, hangs onto your every word! She might stomp out in tears alleging she's never going to speak to you again, but she bounces back *like a boomerang*! She'll even take a telling-off from you more gravely than a bollocking from me! And Heaven knows? I'm always telling her off about something!" It was now the girls' mother was speaking with passion.

"Which leaves our William sitting comfy? Hiding behind the human shield of his wayward sisters?" joked Dad, till Mum shot straight back: "Don't you believe it, Donald! He can be *a little tartar*! *A rascal*! And his wonderful sisters would sooner drop him in the dung as cast their wet wellies in the Porch!"

"You *do* have a remarkable way of expressing things, Eleanor!" was Donald's compliment. "I should have signed you up to do the Clinic's *Talking Therapy* Sessions! You're wasted on Empty Shops!" Here father was talking from the heart, not merely soft-soaping - even less insulting - his long-suffering wife: who didn't, *on this occasion at least*, take his words the wrong way.

"So let's just leave them *to* it?" Eleanor proposed - as if for the last time. "Leave them to stew in their own juice!"

"Ellie!" - Dad hardly ever called his wife 'Ellie' - "Please, please don't let either girl imagine they're in a stew. It's far, far, too early to see their exchange as anything but enlightening."

Luckily, Donald was not cute enough to pick up Eleanor's grunt - nor, in this instance, her cheerful *resignation*.

TWENTY-THREE

As Ophelia stirred the hot chocolate powder into boiling hot milk just before 10 the Monday evening immediately before the Big Swop, she took advantage of finding Mum washing her own *Royal Mail* commemorative *'Postage Stamps of the British Isles'* mug to ask : "Who'll tell Dad about our Swop?"

"I done it – in my own time" replied Mum, "but not a word to *William*.... unless he brings up this amazing plan of yours of his own accord!"

"Which I doubt he will," said Ophelia, " because neither of us are telling him about the swop till it's all safely done with. Not that I think he's *un*reliable," the older daughter continued, "never ceases to amaze me how he'll shut his big hooter for a quid!"

"Too much knowledge!" Mum chimed in. "I'm absolutely certain you'd *never* bribe your brother! Nor would he ever *accept* money to keep his mouth closed.

"Don't you bet on that!" chuckled Ophelia. *"Every man has his price!"*

"Well let's just hope it doesn't come down to buying him off. You *do* know he's quite pally with Candida's Neville: even though they're taught at different ends of the new Millennium Block?"

"Luckily not much will be *visible*. We'd only be rumbled if we were bandaged from head to toe, bleeding, and with bruised faces – or unless Willie wanted to make a point. With 'the Curse,' it's largely *in*visible, to him & Nev - if not for *us*!" Ophelia continued, clutching her tummy.

"Luckily or not, Precious: I'm the world expert on what you call *'the Curse.'* Having not one but two young adults going through the 'wrong-time-of-the-month' informs me *all about* teenage moodiness & tantrums..."

"Thankyou, Mum, for being so understanding," Ophelia gestured. "When we're going through it, I think we both gather you're *rooting* for us."

"Goodnight! Sleep tight!" said Mum as she turned off first the cooker light, then the main spotlights.

TWENTY-FOUR

By Tuesday, with only 72 hours to go, Candida was getting a little nervous – mingled with excitement that she could - & surely *would* - outdo her sister in enjoying Steve's full attention. *But what if the plan was discovered*? What if the swop *itself* crash-landed?

Or what if she was not unwell *enough* on Friday. It was essential Steve didn't see Ophelia, anywhere, on the night itself - or Neville, by chance, see Candida. Whatever paths *normally* collided or coincided would have to be diverged.

But Mandy Tinkerton was still in contention. What had Nev - *or she* - enjoyed going out with him? Had she regretted dumping him? Mandy didn't actually *want* Neville to see anybody else - *or* talk to anyone else? - least of all *Candida* who sustained that long-running disagreement with Mandy over School Council and getting their Poems into the School's brochure; their Short Stories into the once-a-term School Magazine.

And another factor pressed down on relations between the two contemporaries: Mandy's vision of Candida's boobs and peculiar dress-sense? Mandy, inevitably, com*pared* her own appearance and assets with every other girl's. Truth told: Mandy Tinkerton *did* have the capacity to poison Neville against Candida - *or* else pass round gossip, unfounded rumours as well: *anything* to achieve her erstwhile friend's eternal detriment. *And Mandy still commanded powerful allies.*

TWENTY-FIVE

Wednesday October 9th., with still two days to go- but, crucially, with both parents having nearly *a week* to think about the swop: the girls' mother again brought up the subject with Donald : all three of her offspring upstairs doing - *or trying to avoid doing* - Homework.

"If Neville does strike it up with Ophelia, she'll have him for Breakfast!"

"You mean Supper?" Donald corrected his wife, " He'll be *terrified*! She's Deputy Head Girl, for Heaven's sake!"

"Well Neville will be meeting the person, not the reputation!" countered Mum, "Phelia's very kind! Underneath!"

"I'm sure she is! *Sometimes*!" her Dad joked, whilst still wanting to defend his eldest daughter : "Neville can be assured of her best attentions!"

"You mean she'll make the necessary allowances?" said Mum: still wanting reassurance?

"Well maybe the young man doesn't *want* anybody to make allowances for him!" Dr. Donald protested, "from what Candy tells us, he's not had the *easiest* of lives since his mother swanned off. That'll leave him sensitive to anything he thinks is Charity?"

"On that point, you're spot on, Donald!" Mum agreed. "Let's hope he doesn't feel so exposed when he learns of the Experiment that he flees down the road!"

"She's not *that* forbidding!" Ophelia's father repeated-before moving on to the other half - or quarter - of the equation: "*except* with her poor & Younger Sister!"

"Now you really *are* guilty of levity! *I love it!*" cried the girls' mother - with suitable incredulity. "Candy can fight like Cassius Clay! So never call *her* 'poor'!"

"I'll have to accept your judgment!" Donald conceded with mock grudging. "Now we've *met* Stephen in the flesh, and got a better grip on him, maybe it's he who'll be confounded?"

After a few minutes' silence, the girls' mother announced: "You know, I wish them *well*: all four of them this Friday."

"Friday the 11th. : doesn't sound as poetic - *or as fateful* as Friday the 13th ?" father calculated, " I wonder Eleanor? I wonder why they didn't come to me *first*? To confide in *me*. And I *would* have guarded their secret!" Dad's voice now conveyed a little hurt as well as faux astonishment.

"Phelia - *and it was Phelia* - knew you'd probably stamp on the notion. Snuff out the Experiment before it ever caught fire?" elaborated Eleanor.

"If you say so, dear," Dad just squeezed in his customary predication before one of his girls - *he knew not which-* came clattering down the stairs in search of added sustenance.

TWENTY-SIX

"Jammy!"

"What do you mean, 'Jammy?" asked Neville of Sam, 5 minutes before registration on the Thursday morning before the Friday evening of the Swop.

"Easy, please! *Easy does it!*" continued Sam with more than a smidgen of envy: "You and Candy! *It's not fair!*"

"Shut *up*, Sam! You have no way of gauging me - *or* any girl I talk to... It's none of your *business!*" Neville protested.

"Talk to! I bet you do a lot more than *talk to* that bit of toffee?"

Before Neville could reply to this *irritant*: this irritable topic of conversation, this irritable *inquisitor*: another clutch of boisterous Year 11s meandered in: chatting

75

about everything except material they should be studying for their GCSEs.

"*Toffee?* Can *I* have some if it's to spare?" asked Emily as she turned round in her desk to face Sam.

"Sorry I meant Candy: *Randy Candy!*"

"I've told you to *shut up*, Sam! You've said *enough!*" Neville underlined, whilst going quite red in the face.

"Leave him alone, *won't you?*" rasped Emily, leaping to assist Neville.

"That's just what he *can't* do, leave her alone! She's *crumpet!*" persisted Samuel.

"*All stand!*" bellowed Mr. Greaves, Maths Teacher, also their Form Tutor, "And get those hands out of your *pocket*, boy!"

"Yes Sir!"

"I don't know what they taught you in Glasgow, Samuel MacVitie - but it won't do here in *Alderman Cornfield's!* We do things *differently* here!"

Greaves was now in command.

And at this not-too-harsh tutorial reminder, Emily half-turned to wink at Neville who, *very prudently*, pretended he was doing nothing except concentrating on Mr. Greaves' *Daily Notices*.

****

And when during Morning Break the horrible in-comer from North of the Border sidled up to Neville by the Milk Vendor, Candy's boyfriend not only gestured to pat him on the head, but put him firmly in his place at the same time:

"*Glad* you like Candida! Yes she's a girl in a million! I'll let you know how things *progress*!"

"Pro-gress?" Sam chuckled. "I know *exactly* how things will progress. Her knickers will be round her ankles sooner than you can undo your flies!"

Unfortunately for new-boy Samuel, Neville's fair-minded ally Gordon Moorcroft had been listening to the entire exchange. And *Gordon* was Captain of the Under-17 Rugby squad.

Before Sam could escape - perhaps back to *Easterhouse*? - he was inconveniently sprawled across the thin grey carpet - with all the passing girls, *including* a smiling Candida - newly released from English Lit. - expressing   much merriment.

TWENTY-SEVEN

"I'm still *a bit* nervous," admitted a hungry Candida as she got ready at 5-30 on the evening of the Swop, "*Thank Goodness* School today went okay!"

"Well I'm probably twice as nervous as you, Candy!" confessed Ophelia, "because it's a lot more common for a guy to go out with a younger girl than for a girl to go out with a younger lad: *particularly at our* age?"

"Yes some boys are a bit spotty - even scrawny - within our Year Groups. You'd think everyone would mature *at the same rate*?" queried Candida.

"We girls are even ahead on our *Homework*, our Schoolwork - *and our Exams!*" Ophelia confirmed, "*doesn't make sense?* After all, boys are always sticking their hands up, hogging the machines - and bragging how they could march into a GCSE examination room and reel it all out... by simple brain-power!"

"All hat and no cattle!" was Candida's borrowed quotation from their father's *Treasure Chest.*

"Anyway, what are we going to do this Weekend if tonight goes *pear-shaped?"* asked Ophelia.

"I don't think too much *will* go wrong - because we've thought it through - and our programme of activities will probably be miles apart?" was Candida's reassurance.

"Glad you're so optimistic!" Ophelia retorted with some scorn, *"You've* chosen the better straw!"

"Maybe? *Maybe not?"* was Candida's brisk assessment, "we shalln't know till it's all over. In fact, *the Opera's never over till the fat woman's stopped singing!"* Here Candida was again relying on their father's adopted wit.

"What a Sexist Cow, you are!" smiled Ophelia, "I *still* think we ought to have a feather-bed *landing* in mind."

"Easy does it! Cruise *control! You're landing now!"* mocked Candida, trying deliberately to wind her sister up?

"Well how about we go back to *basics?* What I *think* we agreed?" Ophelia responded.

"I've clean forgotten what we *did* agree - or what you agreed with Mum *when I wasn't there*?" Candida's recollection failed.

"It was simple!" cried Ophelia: *"Remember?* No Regrets! No Post-Mortems! No Inquests! *And No Recriminations!"*

"You mean what happens *outside* here stays outside? And what happens *inside* here *stays* inside?" was Candida's summary of her Sister's 4 tenets.

"Indeed!" gushed Ophelia, "So let's all stick to that - and keep our mouths *schtum!"*

"Good Lord!" exclaimed Candida, "it's nearly 6 already and I've so much more to do before Mum gives me the lift she promised at 6-25!"

"Mustn't be late: must we?" was Ophelia's dry observation: words dripping with irony because she herself had far *less* to do. As she herself wasn't the least bit bothered going round the corner for the Bus. *Any Bus.*

ΩΨΩΨΩΨΩΨΩΨΩ

TWENTY-EIGHT

At 6-50 that Friday evening, Steve began to look intently towards Town. Ophelia was notorious for arriving quarter-of-an-hour late for everything. At least 15 minutes. She would quite probably arrive quarter-of-an-hour late for lessons if her teachers did not hold her to account regarding the end of the *preceding* lesson.

When, at the right time, Steve saw *Candida* walking in his direction instead of her sister, he blinked at the spectre and made a friendly: *"Hello there!"*

"Hi! I'm *here*! Hope I'm not *late*? What's *on?"* asked Ophelia's substitute cheerily.

"But... but...." Stephen spluttered: as if his eyes deceived him .

"Its all right, Steve! Ophelia isn't able to get... so she sent me in*stead* - so you wouldn't be disappointed : wasted journey and all that?" Candida explained.

"What's *happened* ?" asked Stephen gravely.

"Nothing's *happ*ened!" continued Candida, " she's just a bit under the weather so couldn't *make* it...."

"*Under the weather?*" Stephen repeated: he still obviously concerned.

"Yes : under the *weather...*"

"*Well then*: I'd better ring her straightway to check that she's *okay*," suggested Stephen, reaching to switch on his chunky mobile phone.

Luckily Candida knew exactly what to say if Steve attempted this: "*Fine!* - But Phelia might be a*sleep*? She might not *welcome* a call that might wake her up?"

"True! I'll text her a bit later, perhaps she'll get it before...?" Steve promised, he now a little more used to the idea that his proper Girlfriend wasn't going to come out of hiding anytime soon.

Still *a bit* dumbfounded, Steve asked: "Do you think it's women's problems? She's not spoken much about that before, but she could have done too much Sport at School or strained something... run out of breath?"

"Well whatever it is, I doubt it's a hospital job - she's simply feeling off-colour.... and unable to rise to the occasion," diagnosed Candida soothingly.

"Which leaves me with you?"

"You could put it that way," responded Candida curtly.

"I could have put that better!" admitted a rather abashed Steve: "I'm de*lighted* you're here! Better than nothing?"

"Thanks a lot! If you're in a hole, stop *digging*! I know I'm not Ophelia - nor am I a parcel the Postman dropped on his round!"

By now, Candida was certain this Swop was a disaster. But then Steve had a moment of enlightenment: "I suppose we *could* just go ahead with whatever I'd planned?"

"*Good idea!*" pronounced Candida: "Let's do just that - and it's bound to be a surprise: because Phelia didn't prepare me - except to say wear something *nice*!"

"And you *are* wearing something nice!" agreed Steve, now somewhat back on track: "That yellow dress is something special. Bright colours suit you... *although...*"

"Although people don't wear bright colours to Funerals..." Candida was determined to finish his sentence, whether or not it was what Steve might have said: " I'm a big believer in re-*claiming* colours! That's why I often wear red: red blouses, red shoes. Other people can do the darker stuff!"

"Men are so lucky!" By now Steve was warming to the theme: "They're expected to go to work in either charcoal grey or dark navy..."

"Not in working-class occupations: *real* workers!" Candida stressed: "You're thinking of posh execs - and stock-brokers: the sort of men *you* encounter!"

Fortuitously, Steve didn't rise to the bait like some helpless bloater. Instead he went into a bit more detail as to his unreformed plans: "What we'll do - *if* it's all right with you - Candida," by now the tone of his voice very solicitous: "is to head for my favourite Gallery, their new Exhibition. *Then* a really exclusive restaurant : *The Florentine*, for a bit of a meal. I know the Owner. *And the Chef*. That's provided you haven't eaten already, Candida?"

"No, I haven't already ate, I mean *eaten*! In fact I *am* rather hungry - but I don't want to put you to all that trouble or expense. A bag of fish-&-chips would well suf*fice*!" Candida claimed, a bit disingenuously because that was more *Neville's* speciality: Neville not being as wealthy as she supposed Ophelia's Steve to be.

"I trust you're not *serious!*" protested a by-now-impatient Steve: "a bag of chips in the back of my *Audi* is not quite my style - nor *Ophelia's!* Let's be off! *Before either place gets busy* - as can happen on a Friday evening. First the Gallery , then the *The Florentine* which should have room for us?"

The two proceeded to walk round the corner to Steve's parked *Audi*, a model only 2 years old. Steve opened the passenger door for Candida, his eyes lingering on Candida's hem-line a moment or two longer than strictly necessary.

TWENTY-NINE

Meanwhile, at exactly 7 o'clock, just before the Church's hollow bell struck 7 times, Ophelia - not *detectably* unwell in any shape or form - turned up to meet Candida's Neville. Therewith she broke her own record by being all present & correct at the stated time.

Except Neville was *not* there - nor was there any lad in the vicinity who might *be* Neville.

"He's always a bit dozy!" Candy had forewarned her sister, "easily gets distracted." Nobody could ever accuse Candida of being *besotted.* She told things as they were - and didn't make excuses either for others - or, in fairness, for herself.

At about 6 minutes past 7, Neville - whom Ophelia had only met 3 or 4 times before, except passing like a ship in the night in a school corridor - ran up to the *Savoy* Cinema's entrance looking flummoxed – *as indeed he was.*

"Good picture on tonight!" Neville gestured: "*Jane Eyre: Franco Zeffirelli!* You evidently wanted to take the opportunity to see it *as well*? Has she gone in to ask about tickets? She's *bound* to be back any minute?"

" *'She'* is the cat's mother!" Ophelia sighed, "There is no 'She' as you put it. *'She'* is not here!"

"Sorry, I don't follow you.. " Neville muttered, "You're saying Candida's not coming to watch Zeffirelli's Jane *Eyre*?"

Neville didn't know the Director of many films. But he *had* heard of Cecil B. DeMille, Ken Russell, and - more prosaically - *Walt Disney*. So like any good scholar, he impressed his teachers by hamming up on factoids

"Correct! She's not *here* - because *'She'* is not feeling very well..."

"Well *she* looked perfectly well at 2-30 afternoon break!" protested Neville.

"2-30 is not *7-30*" Ophelia insisted. "A lot can happen in 4 or 5 hours. Candy told me an hour-&-a-bit ago she was not very clever. *Women's* problems."

Ophelia was secretly quite proud she had managed to keep to the agreed script.

"*Women's* problems," a subdued Neville queried: "I think Marilyn talked about that. She told me her girl Izzy might not be full of beans for three or four days every month. And she *did* mean 'every' month - not just every alternate month."

Ophelia had just enough time to come to terms with the fact that *anyone* would call his mother - or indeed his Stepmother - 'Marilyn,' before grunting: "Now that *would* be a novelty: every *alternate* month!" her voice tinged with sarcasm, "April *down*! May *up*! June *down*! July *up*! *How closely we'll have to monitor my sister Candy's hormones!*"

"Well it's very good of you to come in Candy's place. I just hope you enjoy the *film*!

"Pity Candy's going to miss *out..*"

"Don't be silly! *Jane Eyre*'s been out for *ages*! Candy's quite able to watch the film later, on DVD - or when it's repeated on the telly. The important thing, now, that she feels a lot steadier on her feet."

Poor Neville at this point had no way of knowing his Candida was *not only* perfectly steady on her feet - *but* possibly having a whale of a time with a very wealthy, also healthy, Steve, Ophelia's *usual* escort.

ΩΨΩΨΩΨΩΨΩΨΩΨΩ

THIRTY

In the *"Splash on Canvas"* Art Gallery - packed for the Preview - Candida truly felt she had fallen on her feet. She had spent a great deal of time on her dress and makeup: much to her Sister's consternation. Because, after meeting Steve formally for Sunday Tea a couple of weeks before, she knew she'd have to look her best.

By way of contrast, Ophelia had had to err towards dressing *down* for *her* prospective meeting with Neville, so as not to embarrass him in any way.

Straightway upon entering the heavy glass doors, Divinia the Gallery-owner stepped forward to greet them: "Could your companion - I don't think I've ever *met* your companion? - sign in. Fire regs. & all that!"

Divinia's assistant Zoë came over with a tray of sparkling white wine flutes; one or two equally slender glasses of freshly-squeezed Orange Juice as well. Candida needed no prompt to accept the wine. With satisfaction, she noted Steve chose the Orange Juice instead. "Driving!" he grunted.

"Help yourselves to Canapés!" Zoë waved breezily.

Whereupon Candida expressed delight: "Oh good! *Snacks*!"

"Canapés," Steve corrected her. *Canopies* were something Candida associated with posh buildings rather than posh people & their namesakes; and were *not* items Candida had ever been offered before - except in the marquees of a couple of Weddings where she'd been Bridesmaid. She was relieved Steve scooped four of these wonderful savouries onto *his* shiny-cardboard plate. That gave her tacit permission to help herself to five: prawn, chicken, egg, brie and mini-pizza.

And immediately Candida had downed her first glass of *Prosecco*, she exchanged her empty for a nearby full replacement. Steve, however, and wisely, pretended *not* to notice.

Fifteen minutes later he did, however, comment: "I don't want you tipsy!"

"Chance is a fine thing!" Candida chuckled, "but it really *is* cloudy apple after this!" Then using the throng as cover, she helped herself to another five savouries: each of which she swallowed whole.

"Leave some room for The *Florentine*!" Steve begged.

Was Candida enjoying herself a bit too much? - Steve asked himself as they entered the main Studio to hear Divinia's speech of welcome: short and sweet: paragraphs which ended with her urging everyone to spend a little longer examining the Exhibition: "the highlight of Leeds' Autumn *Culturefest.*"

"Maybe *I'm* the prize exhibit this evening," Candida remarked, "everybody's looking me up and down as if I'm either your daughter, your sister - *or your toy-girl!*"

"And you're *none* of those!" Steve responded decisively, "but friends or acquaintances who know me well might expect a slightly *older* lady companion."

"*Oh dear!* I'm so sorry to disappoint your illustrious acquaintances! They'll have to see me as an aberration, I mean *apparition!*" Candida could put anyone & everyone in their place if she so chose.

At that very moment, a woman 55-ish in sequined evening dress approached the couple: "Good Evening, Stephen... *and* ?"

"*Candida*: sister of her sister," Steve supplied the missing Intro - his borrowed companion wisely resisting the temptation to imitate Lady Muck: "Sister-in-Law of my Sister-in-Law."

"Well sister of your sister: I'm *delighted* to meet you! I trust you'll really en*joy* the artwork on display. Now excuse me: I must catch up with Se*bas*tian!"

"*I really must catch up with Sebastian*," Candida whispered when the woman was out of their hearing. How Candida benefited from that *GCSE* Double-Drama each week...

Within seconds, another lady: at least 6 inches higher than Steve in her high heels, buttonholed him and asked to be introduced.

Steve did this very courteously: explaining that his usual 'friend' - never *girlfriend* - was indisposed, so he'd asked Candida to come in her place.

Candida winced at the word 'asked'- *but he had at least put this Beanstalk off the scent.*

A couple more encounters later, Candida resolved *not* to make herself invisible. "You've got some very *wealthy* acquaintances," she observed in quiet voice.

"Not as rich as they imagine," Steve surmised, "*more arty* than rich."

"I *still* think they've got pots of money!" was Candida's calculation.

"If they have, they wear their affluence *lightly*."

But Candida wasn't going to let Steve off the hook : "Maybe if you're stinking rich - I don't mean *you* in particular - one can *afford* to enjoy big occasions."

"And I'm sure tonight *is* a big occasion. It feels like that to me!" Candida's escort advanced, as he and she shuffled in front of one of the many Canvases that gave this Gallery its name.

THIRTY-ONE

"So when does *Jane Eyre* start ?" asked Ophelia, a little impatiently: she standing on a downtown pavement for quarter-of-an-hour longer than she wanted to stand on a downtown pavement, statue in full sight of curious passers-by.

"In 25 *minutes*: after the adverts."

"*The adverts?*" Ophelia exclaimed, disapprovingly, "whenever I've been unlucky enough to go to a *Multi-Screen* like this, the adverts have been extremely long, extremely loud... and extremely *boring*!"

"Who knows what you might want to buy? - or what films you'd love to see in the future?" Neville asked in his attempt to defend the *Savoy*: "Everything to look forward to?"

"I'm *not* looking forward to the Interlude - or whatever this place calls its commercial break. In fact, they're showing '*FAME*: the Movie'. It'll be starting much quicker! *Any minute!* Have *you* seen '*FAME*,' Neville?"

"No! But I've heard good reports of it. Hot property in the States? Sounds a bit less like English Literature set-text than *Jane Eyre*. Rather more *jazzy*?"

Before Ophelia had chance to comment how the word 'jazzy' sounded *dated*, the girl behind the counter was accepting Neville's £6: "Both at *Alderman Cornfields'*? Two *school*-children for '*FAME*,' Studio 4: front seats only! *Concessionary*."

Ophelia was on the point of choking over this stranger's description of her as 'a school-child.' But held her counsel. Instead, she fished in her bag for three £1 coins to reimburse Neville.

"No! No! No! I pay for Candida most times: when I've done some car-washes"

Ophelia was so astonished getting into *'FAME'* on the strength of a Saturday morning Car-Wash that she merely muttered *"Ta!"* while quickly closing her shoulder-bag; simultaneously pushing against *Studio 4*'s rather heavy door. Into total darkness: *100% darkness.*

Unsure whether she was grabbing other patrons' heads instead of their seat-backs, Ophelia temporarily lost confidence.

"SHHHHH!" *"SHHHHH!"* came shushes from a fairly large - but unseen - patronage, as *FAME*'s Certificate was reproduced for all *except* Ophelia & Neville to see.

Then, by sheer chance, a very light white dance sequence came on *the* screen. Seizing her moment, Ophelia gratefully prepared to slump into the vacant second seat along *Row E*. However, and at the last minute, she hesitated to be seated right next to Neville.

Perhaps she should leave a spare seat in between?

So it was Ophelia dumped only her coat and scarf onto the 2nd. seat in: a seat which promptly bounced straight back into its upright position.

"*SHHHHHHHHHH!*" came more shushes from *Rows F, H, & K.*

"*Sorry!*" said Neville audibly enough for his apology to be heard not only by Ophelia but also by a couple of couples seated straight behind them.

"It's *me* who's sorry!" murmured Ophelia. "Now *settle down* and...."

At that juncture, *FAME* proved more deserving of their concentration than a debate about manners.

THIRTY-TWO

At the Art Gallery, in Handsworth, 7 miles away, Ophelia's sister tried valiantly to know more about Art than she *did* in fact know.

The Exhibition was rather unpromisingly called: '*In the Steps of the Old Masters.*' For those in the know: some rather pretentious 'Modernists' had entered their own creations loosely based on, and 'in the style of,' Tintoretto, Botticelli, Velásquez, whoever - *without ever quite matching their genius.*

When Steve stopped, attentively, in front of any frame, he would, tentatively, ask Candida what *she* thought?

"Right!" she told herself. *"I'll* play the game. *However disingenuously,* I'll teach all these *snobs!"*

Concealed to her sister's boyfriend, Candida *excelled* at *mimicry*: so much so her Mum was known to fall off the sofa laughing when her younger daughter accepted the *Her-Majesty-the-Queen,* the *David-Attenborough* or the *Anthony-Charles-Lynton-Blair* challenge.

And *Ophelia* had long since tired of her room-mate's 'silliness' and her 'showing off:' serving to make Candida *ever more* determined to imitate Willie - *or she.*

Yes, not a few of these Mike Yarwood-inspired arrows had actually landed in Ophelia's compass field: leaving her hurt, *un*amused - and uncomfortably self-conscious.

"Rodinesque!" exclaimed Candida to whoever in *Studio Three* would listen.

"Definitely in the style of Cézanne!"

"Turner*esque*!"

"From the *Gainsborough* School!"

"Cubist? *Yes* I can see quite a lot of Picasso here!"

Every famous painter Candida had ever heard of - most lifted direct from a heavy Coffee-Table book her father had placed in the Lounge - came back to her. Nor could - *or would* - Steve attempt to catch her out: just in case Candy really *did* know her *Art-Decos* from her *Pre-Raphaelites*.

So he drifted into becoming a little more *critical* than she: *not* so openly admiring of the different frames & sculptures Divinia had so assiduously curated.

"Brutalist!" Steve announced, upon seeing a shapeless lump of marble in a perspex case.

"A pale imitation of the finest tradition of *Naïvety!*"

Then the question: "Do you like *this* Japanese watercolour?" Here Steve asking of his charge.

"Well it does show lots of pagodas and water-gardens," was Candida's initial judgment: "very *far-Eastern*!"

Five or six minutes later, Steve was thanking aforesaid Divinia lavishly.

"How *fabulous* you could *both* attend - *and* on our First Night!" their Hostess gushed - whilst taking a last look up and down 'Bimbo' in her fetching sunshine-yellow dress.

Whereupon Candida suddenly decided she needed the *Powder Room*. There she spent 4 or 5 minutes combing her hair before sampling some of different gels, face- and hand-creams on offer. *Real* mini-towels: pure white! Provided for *every* Patron!

Then it was back into Autumn twilight, trailing Steve in the direction of his allotted car lot.

"Did you enjoy that, Darling?" Steve asked.

Did that word *'Darling'* carry any subtle meaning? Candida had to decide. Or was it a rather prim man's expression for *everyone* female?

"Well I emphatically liked the Canopies *and the sparkly*!" she told him, truthfully. *"All very swish!"*

"Yes *Splash on Canvas* does have a certain *pizzazz*! Divinia is marvellous on *Om*-bionce!" agreed Steve.

Leaving the hastening Candida to rehearse that word 'Om-bionce' in order to tease her older sister on the morrow.

THIRTY-THREE

Some miles away, Ophelia - unsuccessfully trying *not* to get bum-ache on rather a hard cinema seat, felt herself distinctly *less* fortunate than her 'little' sister... but that wasn't going to detract from her evening?

The film - even one as engaging as *'FAME,'* gave her precious time to sum up all her doubts - and all her hopes. The boy sat next to her was, after all, *a window into her sister's soul.*

She the undercover agent? *He*, this boy: attempting to live up to her - *or indeed his own* - expectations? *School Child Concession!* Who'd been kidding whom? Ophelia quizzed herself.

Hatching a plan was one thing; not beaching it; not *sinking* it: something entirely different.

Neville was not, routinely, the sort of lad she would have crossed the road for : *too young*, too *immature*, occasionally *gawky*. Of a different generation. *However,* she *did* greatly admire Neville's sister *Isobel.* Izzy the athlete. *Everyone* liked Izzy: knowing Neville and routinely referring to him - as *'brother* of Izzy' - maybe not *real* brother - but a fiercely protective *step*-brother nonetheless.

"I don't want to *upset* him - or her," Ophelia kept telling herself. "It's not worth jeopardizing two perfectly satisfactory situations for a prank. *A prank!*"

The film also gave her longer to think about *Steve. How was he was getting on with Candy?* Or *not* getting on with the indomitable Candy? Had Steve been astonished to see her younger sister arrive at the appointed place? *And was he disappointed? How disappointed?* Or maybe it was *Candy* who was facing the disappointment? *Surely not!* Ophelia concluded. Her Steve was far too polite for that! He'd spoil Little Sissy for sure - *and* without it spoiling *his* evening?

A single word: 'condescending' arose - and kept obsessing the older of the two sisters. Was she herself, *this very Friday* being condescending toward Neville? *Pitying him? Pity* being a type of ritual humiliation? Yes, she'd *have* to be a bit less haughty, a little less supercilious, later that evening? If only to stay faithful to their Experiment....

But would Steve *forgive* her should somebody recognize her - and rat on her? By telling him whom they saw in '*FAME*'? She now a Savoian - a reluctant Savoian? - *admittedly for one night only* : a woman certainly *not* indisposed!

Right now she was beholden to make the best of her lot. To keep *her* side of the bargain.

Ever since she & Candy had planned the Swop, Candy had been a lot more enthusiastic - and a lot more dedicated - to the Project.

Surely her sister would not *steal* Steve from *under her nose*? And surely *he* would not let himself become besotted?

Minutes later, Ophelia told herself sternly that it was *she herself* who'd volunteered; worse *she herself* had gone *to Mum* for her formal blessing! That when she could have simply have snuffed out the Experiment - *aborted take-off* - before it was too late?

Suddenly, Ophelia's reverie was rudely interrupted by a clatter - *and gasp of despair* - to her far Left. A lad and his girlfriend on the other side of the aisle dropped a whole carton full of a ghastly blue iced-liquid: *a slush*. This *supersize* portion now ran down the stairs Olivia had so recently descended: *like a waterfall*.

"Fetch the cleaner!" said girlfriend - overweight and wearing a silver jump-suit - called out.

"Pee off! *You* dropped it! *You* go!"

"S-H-H-H-H-H!" came the renewed chorus from sections of the audience who were enjoying the singing and dancing on screen.

In time, a harassed usherette did bring a wad of dry serviettes from the foyer, recommending these two Sweethearts to move elsewhere ; also to put in for a free *replacement* carton from front of house.

Ophelia was absolutely certain *one* tub was bad enough, let alone *a second*. She surmised this brash couple had not got a smooth path ahead of them: at least not if they spoke to each other so crudely.

"For God's sake, Neville! Don't buy any of *that stuff* for me!"* she rasped under her breath.

Relocated now immediately in front of Neville and Ophelia, the disputatious couple of Lovebirds had evidently not *settled their differences: their only pacification having greater luck with bright* red *liquid instead of blue - but were still arguing about whether to stay or not: because this girl's leggings were sodden.*

"They'll dry out *soon enough*," her intimate hissed.

"You chugging well try wearing wet socks for 2 hours!" the hussy replied. "If *you* hadn't been fishing for a torch, it wouldn't have ended like *this!"*

"S-H-H-H-H-H-H!" shushed an increasingly unhappy audience seated behind Ophelia: convincing her to move another 4 seats even further to her Right, poor Neville trailing behind her. Ophelia did not see why such *ill-mannered* customers should wash their dirty linen in public. It was like enjoying a cup of coffee in *Debenham*'s and being forced to hear the latest episode of somebody's custody-and-access dispute.

From afar, Ophelia could still hear this irascible girl telling her boyfriend: *"Take your stinking change: every penny of it! I don't want it!"*

All followed by *more* commotion - as 15 or 16 pennies and 5p. pieces came cascading down the same steps so recently baptized with blue fizzy.

"Plonker!" cried the overweight girl in silver jump suit.

After another fifteen minutes, *'FAME'* became a more gripping watch. On screen, two *different* sets of young performers were falling in love with each other.

THIRTY-FOUR

"I've known this quaint little restaurant *Florentine* for two or three years. *Quite a find!"* Steve enthused as his *Audi* drew up to the establishment's private car park.

Candida did not think the mile between Gallery and Bistro was worth all the fuss of getting into Steve's car and out again: especially when she noticed - as only a woman *could* - her receding hem-line, also her graceful neck-line, subject to a man's gaze.

"I'm sure they'll fit *us* in!" a disembarking Steve assured Candida: "I know Marco the Maître. Do *you* eat Italian, Candida?"

"I don't know how tasty an Italian *is*?" Here was Candida attempting a joke with somebody who, conceivably, might *not* appreciate her humour: "I didn't have a lot of school dinner today. Stew! Followed by prunes and custard! *Not* our Cook's *finest* hour!"

"So you've got *empty tummy syndrome*," Steve diagnosed.

"Twould have been worse without those *Can*opies!" Candy speculated.

"Candida: they're *can*-a-pés," Steve corrected his charge: which did not go down well when she ventured: "Whatever you call them, they filled a hole!"

"*Bonjourno! Bonjourno* !" Marco greeted his next two customers from behind the wooden mannequin that served to prevent Patrons going straight in. "*Signore, Signora*: a table for two?"

"*Yes*: a table for two *not* next to the window!" was Steve's confident request.

THIRTY-FIVE

"I don't think we've previously had the *pleasure* of entertaining you?" commented Marco, turning toward Candida, "Have you by any chance a twin?"

"Not a twin; only a sister!" which answer Candida was not especially pleased with - because of that dismissive 'only.'

"She's *ill* tonight," Steve apologized.

"Not ill. *Unwell!*" Candida sought to correct her borrowed friend: "A little off-colour."

"Yes, a little off-colour," repeated Steve, tentatively.

"Not *too* unwell, I hope," said Marco as he pulled out Candida's chair, first, and placed a linen serviette on her lap.

"If Ophelia *was* well, there'd be *three of us!*" Steve observed as he began studying the menu, "Then we'd be *a threesome!*"

Luckily, Candida did not read too much into the word 'threesome.' Otherwise their stopover might have been over-&-done-with long before Marco produced his - *or rather his Chef's* - finest.

In the Restaurant's dim light - her lengthy Menu being very shiny - Candida was not at all sure what to order: her predicament worsened by the *Florentine's* exorbitant prices.

"A little drink to start with, Madam?" suggested the returning Marco, as he lit a candle in the centre of the table set alongside the bread sticks

"Pineapple juice, please!" was Candida's request before she remembered how *small* some bottles of 100% juice could be: "Perhaps double, with two ice cubes - *and thoroughly shook up, please!"* Here Candida was happily unaware A) that *Ophelia* might not have been *quite* so specific; B) that Steve might be not a little embarrassed by her telling the Maître how to do his job.

"Just as you wish, Madam!" responded a slightly obsequious Marco. Then turning to Steve: "...and I expect you, Sir, would want blackcurrant & lemon, as usual?" fawned Marco: *"Driving and all that?"*

"But I'm sure my *Companion* would welcome a glass of house wine? Is it So-vee-g-non or Mer-lo?" Steve asked-with poor Candida, opposite, clueless as to whether this question was addressed to her - *or the creep.*

"250 millilitres of anything red would be fine, thanks!" answered Candida after a few moments' awkward silence - and with shocking precision. "They gave us *white* in the Gallery..."

At this moment, Steve was inwardly despairing. Not only had he a young *tippler* on his hands - *wish it were his knee?* - but this Surrogate was definitely *not* a carbon-copy of her older sister!

As Marco shuffled off to fetch said measure - Candida grateful that her glass wasn't going to be titchy - another, even more unctuous, waiter appeared: "Is the lady ready to *order*?" he of the long black apron asked.

"Yes! Minestrone Soup followed by Vegetarian Lasagne, with a mixed side-salad," was Candida's detailed choice: *not* on this occasion lifted from any Menu; simply a repetition of what she'd asked for during a family holiday to Sardinia, two years previous.

"And would Madam like any Parmesan with her Minestrone?" persisted Signor Unction.

"*Cheese?* Yes: two *table*spoons, please!"

THIRTY-SIX

A rather sullen Steve then went on to place his *own* order: one far more faithful to the lengthy, albeit very shiny, Menu still spread out before him.

Candida didn't talk a great deal as she ate - except to compliment Steve on such an extravagant choice of eatery and to hope he wouldn't have to take out a new mortgage to pay for it! At least she did not offer to go halves..... *as she always would* in the company of the sometimes impecunious Neville.

By contrast, Steve used their slow Italian meal to ask Candida 10 or even 11 questions regarding her girlhood, schooling, interests, sporting achievements, musical tastes, whatever: with the exception of two areas he was wise to avoid: how Candy got on with Phelia *day-to-day*; and Candy's *own* menstrual cycle.

And whenever Signor Unction re-appeared - later to bring their profiteroles-with-cream - Candida whispered either: *"They also serve who only stand and wait?"* or *"Bet he wants a tip!"* Neither perspective appealed to her normally unflappable escort who began to wonder whether he could ever safely step into Bistro *Florentine* or, indeed, darken the doors of Gallery *Splashed on Canvas*, ever again?

Then, upon his breaking one of his subjects out-of-bounds: one of Steve's *extra* questions *did* surprise Candida: "I wager you wait on your older sister?"

"I wager *I DON'T* !" Candida protested. "If she wants anything, she can jolly well fetch it *herself*!"

"Perhaps I should be a fly-on-the-wall of your *Room*?" pondered Steve, out loud.

"*And perhaps you shouldn't!*" rejoined Candida in a flash: "You'd be swatted straightaway! Anyway, neither of us can *stand* flies!" countered an increasingly confident Candida, "and we'd thank you for valuing *our privacy*!"

"Well privacy is what we've enjoyed in The *Florentine*," concluded Steve, with not entire accuracy. rather optimistically concluded.

ΩΨΩΨΩΨΩΨΩΨΩΨΩ

THIRTY-SEVEN

Back at *The Savoy*, some couples had come into the foyer already holding hands. And clutches of girls had kissed each other on their way in, like the French do . Neville himself was *not* quite so demonstrative. In turn, Ophelia was not *particularly* warm.

In the middle of *'FAME'*, Neville noted his unscheduled companion: now seated right next to him but probably aggrieved at all the interruptions, had placed her whole body at a skewed angle away from him: neither expecting, *nor wanting*, any physical contact.

"They've quietened *down!*" whispered Neville.

"That's a relief!" Ophelia sighed, taking away the Left hand that had been shielding her Left ear; instead placing it on the seat-arm to her Left. And, deprived of further *free* entertainment, she shuffled until she got herself a bit more comfortable: incidentally bringing her ever closer to Neville.

On screen, Ralph was really falling for Doris. And when Ophelia yawned, Neville stretched out his spare hand till it flopped onto her lap: their first contact. Maybe Nev held *Candida*'s hand on their two previous visits to the cinema as 'an Item'?

Neville had already recognized Candida was not beyond acting schmoozy during a schmoozy film: the couple's hands, *squeezed* hands, conveying intimacy in parallel with the movie's heart-tugging story-line; Candy employing her hands, also, to convey lots of *other* messages? So it was the prospect suddenly struck Neville that Candida's *sister* might welcome the same gesture? *On the other hand, she might not!*

"I'm glad you've given this flea-pit a second chance!" Neville whispered into Ophelia's ear; making her reflect how unusual was Neville's turn of phrase: anachronistic like *'Grub Street'* for Fleet Street, *'Spit-and-Sawdust'* for a pub.

"Pity to waste £6!" whispered back Ophelia: "They should pay *us* £6 for all that commotion!"

Ophelia then had regrets upon remembering how Neville had spent a whole week's pocket money getting them through the turnstile. "Well! It can only get better!" mouthed Ophelia, with more hope than conviction; reflecting she was not *really* up to a *CineTreat* Loyalty Card, *CineTreat* Popcorn, a *CineTreat*

113

Discount, *CineTreat*'s Magazine - or even *CineTreat Prepay.*

What was Candida doing at that precise moment? the older sister asked herself. *Something much, much, better?* Then when more vigorous break-dancing started - U.S. Teens made supple through years of unpaid practice on regimented *Cheerleaders'* quads - *'FAME'* was *very* good: living up to its label: good enough to secure participants' entrance to the *FAME Academy.*

Yes! Ophelia liked these moves. Freed from the awkward pair of Sweethearts - *now safely on their way home?* - Neville's companion became quite *engrossed* in celluloid relationship-building: *not* engrossed enough, however, to respond positively to Nev's hand when it strayed over the arm rest.

An accident? She tried to be charitable. But each time his wiry Right hand appeared, Ophelia sat more huddled, pretending to *ignore* him.

'FAME' foreshadowed increasingly popular T.V. quizzes like *Weakest Link,* much later *Pointless* or *Dancing on Ice*: based on the successive *elimination* of Candidates: 8, 7, 6, 5, 4, and so on till a clear Winner weeps

uncontrollably upon hearing the judges' verdict. No, Ophelia *didn't* want that tired formula. Instead she told herself she'd warm more to *Cinema Veritas*: *Love Among the Haystacks* - or *Saturday Night and Sunday Morning*.

THIRTY-EIGHT

"Good Heavens! It's 9-30 al*ready!"* Candida exclaimed while looking at her watch in the dim light. "I'll have to ring Mum to say I'll be late! *Is that all right?"*

"Do go ahead!" Steve encouraged her, "from what I've seen, she's the sort of mother who'd *welcome* reassurance? And could you ask her how *Ophelia* is progressing in her bedstead?"

"As long as Mum hasn't got to turn out in the dark to *fetch* me!" Candida jested, with more than an inkling of sincerity. *"I'll say 10-40-ish!"*

"-ish," reiterated her Companion of Honour.

"Will do!" answered Candida as she hastened to the *Ladies* and pressed the 'Mum' button on her new

phone's address book. *"By the way:* Steve's asked me how my indisposed sister is getting along?"

"A bit better? Good!" Candida stressed before switching off her phone and putting it back in its zipped-pouch.

Seconds later, she was *about* to report back the good news to Ophelia's *usual* man-friend when that other turd Marco came up to their table: "I do trust Madam is not feeling un*well*?" he asked of Steve.

"No! My young friend decided to make her brief call *away* from the table: that she might abide with your preference that telephones be neither employed *nor responded to* in the Bistro itself," Steve elaborated.

"Well we *do* make *occasional* exceptions," conceded the obsequious Marco, doubtless fearing for his gratuity.

The couple now alone again, Steve reassured Candida: "I really *will* deliver you safely to your front doorstep..."

"And bedstead!" Candida quipped. "You know? It feels so strange - discovering someone *rich* enough to own a car of his own!" Here she drew breath: "Though I must say, my *usual* boyfriend would never let me go off

unless he walked every *inch* of the way - or *personally* delivered me to my Dad's car," Candida made plain.

"In any case, Mum says she must always know where I am *however late I am*. To-night she says I'm in *good* hands."

Nobody knows exactly what was in Candida's escort's mind upon hearing this. He merely paid up, plus tips all round - which Candida did *not* offer to contribute towards - *and left*.

THIRTY-NINE

Back home, the telephone sounded loud and insistent.

"Bet it's one of the girls!" Eleanor Crabtree guessed.

"Settle down! Let it ring!" responded Donald: "When was the last time either of them rang from a date to tell us how they were getting on?"

"But... *but*..." Mum looked flustered.

"Eleanor: is it *snowing* outside?" her husband asked, knowing the answer already because this was simply a

117

dull, occasionally starlit, Friday evening in October. The Doctor - he always downplayed the 'Doctor' bit, lest people thought he was a G.P., or worked in a *hospital* - was not unknown to bring red herrings into a discussion or conversation: treacle when talking about politicians; labour camps when talking about call centres; cowboys when talking about elections. That perhaps explained his reference to *snow*.

Mrs. Crabtree always said his mind was in overdrive: darting from one subject to another just like all of his teenage patients with ADHD!

When the phone rang *again* – now more persistently - the girls' mother bolted into the corridor to answer it. And with a sigh, Dad threw his *Guardian* on the floor and stood behind the slightly-open door to listen in.

Perhaps it was *Candida* on the other end of the phone? Whoever it was, Dad decided Eleanor sounded very patient: not always her telephone manner, sharpness getting the better of her when being pestered by one of their three children. *Yes*: she loved all three something cruel; but that did not prevent her snapping at them if she thought they were being stupid - *or too* demanding...

"Yes"

"No"

"Indeed!"

"No."

Far from putting Donald off - and sending him back to his armchair - these uninformative affirmatives tempted Dad to eavesdrop even *more* attentively

"No"

"Perhaps?"

"3 O'clock"

"Well, if that's all right with you...?"

"I'll mention it to his Father"

"Thankyou for letting me know. Goodbye!"

"And what was *that* all about?" Donald asked his wife, *casually*, upon her re-entry to the Lounge... pretending he'd been reading his Paper all the time...

"Something wrong with William?"

"Donald: have you been *listening?*" Mum asked accusingly, "It was actually the Scout Leader confirming William's next slot for Archery Practice.... *a week to-morrow...*"

FORTY

"Fancy some pie and chips?" Neville asked Ophelia as his surrogate girlfriend emerged from the *Savoy*'s Rest Room, "Candy & me: we've found this brill Pie shop! He makes his own; 7 different types: Steak & Kidney, Steak-&-Onion, Beef Mince in..."

"Thankyou, Neville," Ophelia responded wearily, "I get the point. Fetch me Cheese & Bacon or 5-bean vegetarian when we get there! And just a *half* of a baked potato, with butter only, not a *whole* potato. *You* can have the other half, Neville! Perhaps it'll not be so *dry* if we share a *whole* potato?"

"Fine! Won't be more than 5 minutes.. *and* I'll get you a clean fork..." Before Ophelia had chance to say that she certainly *expected* her fork to be clean - *& wrapped in*

cellophane - Neville disappeared inside the brightly-lit *Proctors' Pie Shop.*

And being a fairly balmy Autumn evening, Ophelia sat on the triangular bench of the small play-area where 2 main roads met.

Neville kept to his word and reappeared remarkably quickly. "You're *lucky*! *Last Cheese-&-Onion pasty in his oven*!" At this happy outcome, the boy passed Ophelia a small polystyrene box together with plastic spoon, *wrapped.*

Unfortunately for their "date" : when Neville, conscientiously, divided one enormous spud into two *half*-spuds, the whole very-hot hot-potato rolled on to the gravel beneath their bench.

"*Oh dear!* One for the *Pig*eons!" gasped Neville. "But wait on! I'll fetch a bag of crisps in*stead*!"

And before poor Ophelia could haul him back, upon her determination she was no keener consuming salty crisps with her Pie than retrieving the baked-to-order potato now lying beside her right foot.

"*No thanks, Nev!* No crisps for *me...* but this Cheese Pie's *mouth*-watering, certainly not over-cooked!" Here Ophelia was far too accommodating to share with Candy's friend knowledge of what food, or foods, *Steve* accessed for her benefit. Normally.

Then, just as the couple rose to *Keep Britain Tidy* - also to retrieve stand-in sister her beauty sleep - Ophelia was aware of giggle & chatter she was definitely *intended* to hear from the nearby bus-stop.: "*Look at her!* Deputy Head Prefect with a lad just out of *nappies*! How she's come down in the world: *hasn't she*?"

"*Millicent!*" Neville called across, using the longer form of Millicent's name Millie in order to get under her skin: "*Millicent!* Can't you accept Candida's un*well* tonight? Otherwise she'd be here for our Foursome?"

"*Foursome!* How I'd like to join a *foursome!*" exclaimed Millie's friend Tracy: same year, different Comp. "*Watch out, Missus!* You don't know what he's capable of?"

"*Not a lot!* In fact very *little*! Hee, hee!" Millie chimed in, provocatively.

"*Hee, hee!*" repeated Ophelia, limply, under her breath, "rather more than *you* sluts imagine...".

"Go and jump in the River Aire!" a frustrated Neville suggested, just as the *Number 93* Bus opened its front door to whisk Millicent and Tracy off to their sleepover.

"Cretins!" was Neville's description of the pair to a still unimpressed Ophelia.

FORTY-ONE

Back at *"Clovelly,"* Eleanor Crabtree felt inwardly vindicated worrying about her two girls during their risky swop: *"Stop kidding, Donald*! You're *just* as much on the edge of your cushion *as me*! Phelia and Candy have, maybe, bitten off more than they can *chew*?"

"They've made their beds *and can lie in them,*" Dad quoted, with a note of resignation.

"Holy heliports! I trust you're *joking,* Donald!" the girls' mother continued, "The *last* thing either girl should be doing is taking a boy into their *bed*! However *nice* the boy! However well-protected! I've discussed *that* subject with them. With *both* of them! *No holds barred!* And I've even threatened them that if either of them's ever caught under *this* roof - or any other roof...."

"You'll dis*own* them..." her husband helpfully finished her sentence off: to his wife's *visible* discomfort.

"Come to think of it, Donald? I *wouldn't* disown them. *Even though* they'd led some poor lad astray..."

"Or con*ceiv*ably, an extremely con*tented* lad could have led one of our *extremely willing* girls astray?" argued their Dad, adding rather mischievously: "backed a *winner*?"

"Donald! How *could* you? I want you to *stop* these crudities! It's no *joke*! You *of all people* should be debunking all those myths about boys coming to the well and taking their fill! *Receiving their rations*! Don't you *realise:* it's incumbent on lads to make a *lifelong* commitment? I should be *just* as angry with *William* in five years time: if *he* got some girl into trouble"

"That joy's still to *come!*" predicted Dad.

"You're at it *again* Don! *Double meanings!* Yearning to re-enact some tribal custom where a man and woman do it in front of the Altar, to consummate their vows?"

"*Darling!* You've been reading far too much Anthropology! I can just imagine *our* Minister's reaction if *we* had done it: right there and then, and in front of the whole congregation. Sowing *good* seed in the furrow…?"

"That's quite e*nough, Romeo*! I'm off now to get us both a large mug of tea - and when I come back I'd be *extremely* grateful if we could put sex - and *all* our hang-ups about sexual congress - to one *side*!"

"*Right-ho!* Off you go!"

And back, immersed in his Crossword, the good Doctor could hear the telephone ringing *again.*

FORTY-TWO

Simultaneously: and in the private *'Patrons Only'* yard to the rear of *The Florentine*, Candida felt emboldened enough to speak concerning the possible *downside* of tipping: "I think tipping is *humiliating.* It degrades both the giver *and* the receiver?"

"But Gratuities *do* have the joint advantage of letting Waiters and Waitresses know they're ap*prec*iated. Also boosting their *pay*," objected Steve.

"Too true!" gasped Candida, "they're paid a miserable pittance; and tipping *supports* that shocking inequality... And I bet some wicked Managers pocket *even the tips*, let alone the proper wages they should have paid in the *first* place!"

"Golly! You're quite a *tub*-thumper!" responded Steve, with a voice not entirely free of faint praise.

"Yes I *am*, Ste-phen! - *and proud of it!*" boasted the surrogate, "...and what's more? In two years' time I'll vote for *any*body, any Party, who remembers the poor *at the gate!*"

"*Please*! Let's not discuss politics on such a beaut-i-ful evening," begged Steve, "I'm sure we shan't find *Marco* slumped at the gate!"

"Glad for *his* sake!" was Candida's final, sarcastic, contribution to a very interesting debate. Then, quiescently, she got back in the front passenger seat of Steve's car, *this* time swivelling round towards the steering-wheel as she did so: in the process defeating her escort's scarcely-suppressed leer.

ΩΨΩΨΩΨΩΨΩΨΩ

FORTY-THREE

"I'll walk with you, Phelia. To the outside of where you live. I do that for Candy *without fail!*"

"I'm sure you do!" Ophelia answered, as the pair began their rather round-&-about journey 'home.'

Just as the pair passed the dark *Southside Primary School* surrounded by its new prison railings, Ophelia halted. And asked her junior: "Neville: do you want me to *kiss* you? My way of thanking you for the film and the Pie... *and your company*?"

"No it's all *right!*" Neville responded, "*Candy* might be upset. Besides me and she don't do too *much* of that till we've been going out a bit longer. Izzy told me *to bide my time.*"

"I'm *sure* she *did*, Nev. Sisters are there for guidance? And you're certainly *not* doing anything *wrong* accepting a peck on the cheek from someone you can trust... someone who just wants to say *Thankyou!*"

"Well, *all right!* As long as you're not upset about those squawking girls and that ruined baked potato?"

"Silly boy!" Ophelia tut-tutted as she drew her lips towards Neville's lips.

And that was the cue for Neville to lock his jaws as tightly as a swimmer's.

"Relax! *I'll* tell you how to do it!" smiled Ophelia, "Open-up!"

"Well if that's what you want?" whispered a clearly startled Neville.

Within seconds he could experience the tip of Phelia's soft tongue in his mouth touching the tip of his own tongue. Unconsciously, he let this happen just long enough to discover its delight, whilst *still* not allowing *his* tongue to stray inside *her* mouth.

"Gosh!" he said after those 19 or 29 seconds of bliss: "that was nice. *Really nice!* Not what I'd ever do with your sister! *Wouldn't dare!* Good job I didn't order garlic-*coated* wedges!"

"Sleep well, Phelia!" he said when the pair reached her gate, not very far from *Southside Infants'* as the crow flew. *"And give my love to the Outpatient!"*

"Will do!" promised Ophelia at her front door, secretly confident said Outpatient would still be out!

FORTY-FOUR

"Before I take you home: that short run," Steve prevaricated: "I should very much like to show you Jedediah Boult's *New Mill*: one of the 1st in the world to produce high-quality worsted wool!"

"We won't see much of it at this time of night?" Candida noted.

"Nevertheless, it's still worth your seeing such a beautiful *restoration*: facilitated in great part by the *Leeds Archaeological Society* of which I'm a member," Steve contended.

And when they got to the end of a long gravel track, the *Mill* complex's outline could just be seen against the Moon: *in silhouette*.

Stopping the car, Steve lit up the *Mill's* 250-year old stonework with his full-beam headlights.

"Well it looks a wreck to me!" was Candida's observation: she clearly *un*impressed, "I should pull it down & spend the money on something *worth* saving!"

"This *is* worth saving!" protested an injured Steve.

"*As you wish!* There's no accounting for some people's *hobb*ies!" was Candida very casual appreciation.

"*Vocations!*" Steve sought to put the record straight.

"I've only ever heard that word '*Vocation*' used for *Priests* - except what our Prime Minister calls interior *decorators!*" intercepted Candida.

A few moments of silence followed while Steve stealthily turned off his car lamps. *All of them.*

"I don't *like* this!" gasped Candida, she a little worried, "*It's creepy !* Can we go *home* now?"

"Indeed! I'm sorry I shouldn't have tried to fit in a diversion. I merely thought you'd be intrigued to witness the Society's *progress*?"

Before Candida could reply, Steve did turn on his sidelights - and fiddled with the fan setting, also with his de-mister, situated toward the extreme left of his dashboard; when accidentally, or on purpose, his floppy hand rested on Candida's stockinged knee.

"*Get off!*" cried Candida, "I don't know what you do with my sister? And I don't *want* to know... and I'm sure

130

you're always as nice to her as you've *tried to* be to me tonight."

That *'tried to'* stung Steve   as assuredly as his companion *intended* it to be stinging: "What's good enough for Ophelia should not be lesser for her sister?" he spluttered.

"I do not, however, want *your* hand - or any other man's hand - on my knee!   *Nor* do I feel entirely *safe* in the middle of nowhere!"

"So *sorry* Candida!   I could *see* you were a bit scared. I just wanted to reassure you I'm still here for you in the dark. Also to say *'Thankyou'* for this evening," Steve whimpered.

"Your best way of saying *'Thankyou'* is to turn that engine on, and head straight back to *Clovelly*," Candida replied with veiled anger.

"At first, I was a bit *crest*fallen to learn of Ophelia's illness..." explained Steve as he gently revved up the engine.

"Her monthly" Candida interrupted "her Curse... and I always accept thanks, *and I want to thank you too* - but please do *not* show your thanks by attempting to *molest* me!"

"That's where I *can* reassure you..." began Steve in faltering response.

"Well, at present I do not *feel* reassured," Candida objected, "a plumber my Dad knew came to service the boiler on one of my Inset Days and asked me to mend the zip of his flies - whereupon I threatened to ring 999. *He* said 'sorry:' his zip had been missing a tooth a bit earlier. I said: 'You'll be missing *a lot more* than a tooth *if my Dad finds out what's in your mind!*' "

"Well you need have no worry regarding *my* plumbing," was Steve's feeble attempt to regain Candida's confidence.

Back home, her escort could not resist seeing her out of the car, in person, 'so that her best shiny blue shoes were not trapped in the gutter?' Perchance, *near*side, Steve could take one final look at Candida's *bosom*?

"I won't come *in*," Steve gestured: not that Candida would *invite* him to enter. "I'd only wake Ophelia *up*!"

"*And* wake Mother!"

"Maybe Phelia's already spotted us from the top window?" a dilatory Steve hoped.

Candida prayed not!

"Tell her I'll be in contact in the morning," requested the lingering Steve, slowly re-opening his driver's door.

"*Not too early!*" Candida whispered, "it *is* a Saturday."

"*Right-ho!*" agreed Steve as he stole one last glance up to the 'Penthouse.'

Driving off, the older man doubtless reflected how just or justifying herself having such an eventful *and tipsy* a surrogacy?

But after courteously waving Steve off, Candida knew three things perfectly well: A) that her sister Ophelia would have got back considerably *earlier* than she. Wouldn't it be awful if *all four* had met outside *Clovelly*? B) that Mum would *not* be in bed; & C) that she need never fear Mum -or Dad's -wrath, herself now as sober as a judge: unlike her *older* sister who had once got herself grounded for hiding a whole bottle of *Lambrini* in their fitted wardrobe.

FORTY-FIVE

"Hi Mum! *Thanks for staying up for me!*" said Candida chirpily as she entered the Lounge where the late *News & Papers* were still on the telly.

"Of *course* I'm up! Even if you DO have a key! And thank you to *you* for ringing us from the Restaurant. *Very considerate!*" Candida's mother commented warmly. "I'm *sure* you've been all right...? *And in very good hands!*"

Candida resisted the temptation to say anything more whatsoever regarding 'hands' and asked quite innocently: "Am I earlier than *Phelia*?"

"Gosh, she's been in *an hour-&-a-quarter*! And she looked to be re*covering*," Ophelia's mother reported.

Again Candida showed remarkable restraint not asking for any more clarity reference that word 'Recovery'. "Doubtless, she'll tell all *to us all* in the morning...?"

"*Goodnight, Cherub!*" bade Mum cheerily.

"*Goodnight, Mum!* I'll be close behind you on what Dad always calls 'the wooden hill.' "
"Just switch off the bottom passage lights."

FORTY-SIX

On the first floor, Candida slipped into the Guest Toilet & sat to read Neville's 3 texts: *just like him* to send 3 not one, she told herself!

Text One: 19-25
<< SORI U'RNOT WEL.GETWELSOON! NEVX >>

Why did Nev always write in Capitals? Candida queried. And his *stupid* Service Provider: charging *by the character*!

Text Two: 21-11
<<MUSTELU: O'S MAGIC! GOOD CUMPNY-BUTNOT ASGOODASU!LVNEVXX>>

Text Three: 22-58
<<PING'LL WAKEU UP!SORRY! GETBETTA! MISTU! BEDTIM!C.U!NEVXXX>>

In the ensuing moments: Candida - uncomfortably perched on the wooden lid of the Guest Toilet - in sheer frustration pressed DEL/DEL/DEL, before rattling her phone's *START* Button till it stopped lighting up - & gasped *sotto voce*: "Stupid boy! Sorry! *Very* Sorry! *My backside!*"

And this younger daughter in pretty sunshine yellow dress, now a little crumpled, *would* be ascending the final flight of stairs to her own bed *but for seeing* a bright light in the pitch dark shining in the gap beneath her brother William's door.

FORTY-SEVEN

Candida   gently knocked twice on her brother's NO ENTRY Door & entered : much to her brother's astonishment, but *not* his annoyance.

Fearing she might tell him off for reading so late, he whispered: "*Nearly* finished this Chapter! Is my light *that* bright?"

"No! Not at all! *I'd* read late if I had a Bedroom of *my own!*" Candida answered with not a little yearning. "No, William: I need you to keep *a secret*, a very big secret; a very important secret! Can you do that?"

"As long as I don't have to *fib*! Dad's always going on about fibbing! If you tell one porkie, you need *another* porkie to cover up the 1st. porkie!"

Cue inner amusement on Candida's part that little Willie was adopting Cockney rhyming slang: Pork *Pies*.

"No I shan't ever ask you to fib. Nor will *Phelia* ask you to fib. She's in this *with* me - and I'm certain she would not want you to fib - simply stay *quiet*!"

"*Oh I get you now!*" a tired William came to life and propped himself up a bit higher on his double pillow, "that's another thing Dad said at one of our Conferences: the sin of *omission*! And I remember thinking *fancy it being a sin not to say anything*?"

"Well it *is* a sin if you see a car crash or a beating-up - worse a knifing - and you *don't* come forward; but the silence I'm asking for isn't that bad. *Not really!*" Candida clarified.

"Is it to do with your being late in tonight?" asked William, "*are you in trouble?*"

"Amazingly: *No!*" his sister chuckled, "It's just that I spent the whole evening this evening with *Phelia*'s Steve - and *she* spent the entire evening with my Nev!"

"*Never!* That would never, *ever*, work!" speculated a clearly baffled William, "you can't do a swop as easy as that! You'd be *rumbled*?"

"Well we *did* do a swop! And maybe suc*ceeded?*" Candida here careful to eliminate doubt from her qualified enthusiasm. "And Phelia told Nev, and I told Steve, that we'd both got '*women*'s problems' - which luckily is *true* - because we're both women - and we're both living through the month of October!"

"Yes! For 2 or 3 days each month, I keep out of your way when one of you is ratty - but you're not *always* ratty!" William conceded.

"I'm sure we're not!" agreed Candida.

A pause for breath.

"So what we're asking you to do, Willie, is simply to stay very quiet, very innocent. *Both* your sisters have different reasons - *or rather the same reason* - not to be able to see their respective Flames on one chosen Friday. *Understand?*"

"I think I can do that?" promised William, whereupon Candida leaned forward to kiss his forehead: a gesture he always feigned to be embarrassed by; not that his discomfiture was anything other than *fleeting*.

138

"Good night!" whispered Candida as her brother reached to turn off the same light that had attracted her to venture in, in the first place, *"and Thanks!"*

FORTY-EIGHT

Upstairs in the 'Penthouse,' Candida brushed her teeth in the dark, laid her best sunshine-yellow dress on the back of what might be a chair, then changed into the soft *David Nieper* nightdress Phelia had given her last Christmas.

And buoyed up by how *nice* everyone had been: Steve, latterly; Mum; then Willie, she was resolute not to get into any discussion *or* analysis *or* post-mortem with her somnolent sister.

Or was Phelia only *pretending* to be asleep? To surprise this latecomer with a barrage of questions? Who had come away from their Experiment the better? Who was the luckier?

And would the fizz, the buzz, *last*?

Perhaps the hard work was only just beginning? To get all four participants - two of them not a little surprised-back into rôle, back to normality? Or had Candida *herself* opened a can of worms by not pressing the 'Abort' button?

Soon there was a bit more streetlight in the Upper Room, prompting Candida to gently kiss Phelia on the cheek before herself dropping asleep in the 4-foot bed positioned opposite.

FORTY-NINE

Neither girl was up-and-about early on the Saturday morning. But as they washed and dressed, warily glancing in each other's direction, suppressing any temptation to begin exchanging details: they heard a door-bell ring loud & clear.

Mum, fully ready for the day, was answering the door. Only *Consignia* deliveries came that early.

Leaning over the banister in curiosity, Ophelia picked up the visitor's odd words:

"Sorry she's not clever...."

"Can I leave these Michaelmas Dai... our Garden?"

"Would invite you...

"All right... thanks lots Mrs. Crab..."

"Who *was* it?" Candida asked, as she emerged, almost naked, from their shower.

"Neville"

"*Neville?*"

"Neville: *I think.*"

"It was either him or *not* him?" exclaimed the younger girl, drying herself down.

"And what did he *say*?" inquired Candida.

"Not sure? But he might have brought you a box of Paracetamol ... *and a cucumber*?"

"*Stop being silly!*" Candida cried out.

"Might have been a *marrow*?"

"Phelia: the way your mind *works*! You're simply winding me *up*! *And I don't like it!*" Candida whined.

Over breakfast, both girls were guarded -as if neither knew what to say next... *which was unusual.*

"Well you *do* look happy, the pair of you..." Mum observed, "Yet Candida: you were walking *on air* last night!"

"*That's good!*" Ophelia responded curtly: "I notice you fail to say that *I* came in happy as well!"

"*True!*" ... but before Mum could elaborate, a triumphant Candida interjected: "*Misery*-guts here is only grumpy because she thinks I drew *the luckier straw!*"

"That's what *you* think, Candy!" objected Ophelia: "*Just you wait and see!*"

"I *can* see!" Candida claimed. "*I* got a bunch of flowers to comfort me in my illness, helping me to become *well* again!"

"Bet you *I'll* get the best bouquet in the world when Steve brings it round!" was Ophelia's stated hope, "At least he won't pick *dandelions* from the grass verge outside his house!"

Then: just while Candida was rearranging Nev's Michaelmas daisies in their adopted *Portmeirion* vase - she determined not to cry - Mum intervened: *"Now Ophelia!* That was a very un*charitable* thing to say. The lad gave us his all: like the widow's mite. I want you to *apologize!"*

"Sorry, Sis! I was unkind. Do you for*give* me?"

Before Candida could issue perfect absolution, a jaunty William came into the kitchen and headed straight for the Cona Coffee.

"I overlay! Can't think *why*? P'raps it's because it's a Saturday?" And while he thought about it, Candida winked at him. *No risk of his acknowledging their late-night tryst?*

"Fancy *both of you two* invited out last evening!" William grinned, "wish some pretty girl would invite *me* out for a walk round the lake?"

"No fear of that!" grumped Ophelia.

"Far from it," Mum intervened again, "in a couple of years William will be *Belle of the Ball*: all those young ladies clustering round him!"

"Well before that happens, he'll have to buy a suit from *Burton's the Tailor*," suggested Candida, "he *lives* in that *Leeds United* track suit. He'd wear it all night if I hadn't spent all my pocket money last Christmas buying him *Leeds United* 'jamas!"

Candida smiled again at her brother: which struck her sister as a bit odd - because it was normally *Candy* bitterly complaining that her brother got 'all' the available second-helpings: the same left-overs Dad dished out to him under that perpetual pretext: "*Hollow legs, you know?*"

"Fancy *both* of you having boyfriends: very rich boyfriends who can keep you in the style to which you are accustomed!" Here William was quoting from some '*Upstairs, Downstairs*' episode he'd heard on classic revivals.

FIFTY

"*Nobble Steve! I should!* He's dripping with money - and I *bet* he hands a dollop over to Phelia?" It was now evidently *Candida*'s turn to speak an untruth.

"He does *not*! Anyway Steve's income is quite modest - *nor* do I have any desire to sponge off him!" was Ophelia's indignant response: "I *always* pay my own way - *except when Steve's been washing other folks' cars and got paid for it...*"

Amazingly, none of the three others round the breakfast table picked up on this daring allusion - or *if* one of them did, he or she was definitely not going to call out what Phelia might be referring to.

"Good job Dad bought us all that doorstep of a book: '*A Complete Guide to Victorian Masterpieces,*' " continued Candida determined to add to the other three's bafflement. " You never know when you'll be asked to comment on the merits of Edward Byrne-Jones and the early Cubists?"

"You mean *Rubik's Cube*?" asked William, warming to the theme.

"Anyway, if you'll excuse me, I'll just pop upstairs to finish off...before" said Ophelia, rising from her chair this time *without* sharing glances with Candida.

"Before you do the upstairs' *Hoovering*!" Now it was *Mum* helpfully completing her elder daughter's sentence, "as it's *your* turn this Weekend."

"And so it is!" was Ophelia's abrupt assent, careful as she was, today, *not* to grumble, because *somebody* had to wield the noisy *Vactric.*

The whole family were off to their caravan near Barmouth the Friday afternoon of the following week: *Half-term holiday,* so there'd be little time - *one single Friday evening* - for 'normal service' to resume : Ophelia with Steve, Candida with *Neville.*

That did not stop Ophelia taking 55 minutes out, on the 1st. Sunday evening after the swop, to grill Steve, over his landline, as to how he'd got on? Preferably, after checking out no listening *ears* behind the door?

And *already* she'd received that beautiful bouquet of flowers she'd anticipated: dutifully delivered by Steve, he in turn so gratified to hand them over *personally* to her soon after Sunday Dinner's washing-up. *Between* Friday and Sunday, he'd actually written Ophelia a very lengthy - and charming - text:

<< Ophelia, my Darling! How downcast I was when I learnt you were unwell the other night. These illnesses can be quite troubling. Unlike you to be under the weather. And you were sorely missed. Never quite the same without you. Your sister Candida did however fill in

for you admirably. It was so kind - & self-sacrificial - of you to send her in your stead. You are fortunate indeed to have a sister like she! Affectionately yours, Steve. >>

And Ophelia had been very, *very* careful not to press DEL. by mistake. In fact she re-read Steve's well-meant Text often enough to pick holes in it. Steve was laying it on *a bit thick* with his *'illnesses'*; also why the *'sorely missed'*? Did her man *really* mean it? Also his word: *'admirably'*: what did that mean in truth?

Had Candida taken up the assignment a little *too* keenly and enjoyed herself *too* much? *Or* had she used the opportunity to cross-question Steve about what her older sister did on other occasions? *What* family or 'Penthouse' confidences were betrayed? Could Candida *really* be trusted not to flirt with Steve? *After all*, she knew how to wind *her father* round her little finger?

None of this reading into Steve's text - nor his beautiful, nay *extravagant*, bouquet - persuaded Ophelia to ask Candida directly 'what happened?' And she *certainly* was not going to give the wretchèd girl sight of Steve's text. *None of her business!* Besides, would Candy hand over *her own* Mobile: the one containing all *Nev*'s sweet nothings? *No! No! No!*

147

The only time *Candy* spoke directly concerning that Friday: which *could* have broken their prior *'No Inquisition!'* - *'No Post-Mortem!'* - *'No Recriminations!'* agreement was when she reassured her sister that brother Will was necessarily *in* on the swop: he given minimum feedback possible   so that he didn't, *unintentionally*, drop these two Flames - his two guides and mentors - metaphorically in whatever puddle might snuff out those fires of desire. *Forever?*

That recognition made *Ophelia* a lot happier. Otherwise poor William might have opened the door to one or other 'lad,' and unwittingly contradict their *'Women's Problem'* alibi. As for Mum & Dad, thank Goodness they, too, had been dragged into the plot. Conceding only that oft-repeated understanding: 'no *fibs* would be told?' Nor should menstruation *automatically* interfere with their daughters' social - or academic - lives.

FIFTY-ONE

Monday, an ordinary school-day for Candida: double Maths, followed by double Combined Science; then *after dinner*: single Religion, Double English Literature. *Not* her favourite day, because of the Chemistry Lab -

but an exciting opportunity to see Neville for a precious 10 minutes after *his* Canteen Sitting.

"Hope you're fully *better,* Candy?" inquired Neville solicitously, "you got me really worried: you too *ill* to turn out. Not like you?"

"Just *women's problems!*" Candida explained breezily, *"Izzy'll tell you all about it!"*

"Good job your sister was in such fine fettle!"

"Yes I felt it important you shouldn't be *stood up!*" Candida further explained.

"You're not the sort of people to dump me!" Neville commented truthfully, "you would have rung me before I set out! I *know* you would."

"I've never really taken to that word 'dumped' " admitted Candida, "and I know *you'd* always tell me before I was stuck outside some God-forsaken Cinema."

"Had a *good* choice of Film actually, *in the end. FAME! Do* get hold of it on Video or DVD!"

"Yes set-text *Jane Eyre* on a Friday evening *is* a bit like Schoolwork" Candida concurred.

"But it was the Zeffirelli *re*-make!" Neville sparked up, still proud that he could name-drop 4, maybe 5, famous Directors.

At that precise moment, Mandy & Natalie deliberately made it their job to happen to pass that corner of the tennis court: "Who's a lucky *boy?*" Mandy chirped, not expecting an answer, *only a glare* - from her rival Candy's steely eyes.

"Hooked his Deputy Head Girl! Clever!" chimed in Mandy's equally obnoxious sidekick Natalie Parsons.

"Looking *everso* grown up: he was in his short trousers!" Mandy continued her taunts.

"Did he have *any* trousers on, I wonder?" Natalie asked whoever would listen.

"Push off, Fag-ash!" ordered a statuesque Neville: "Just because Ophelia caught *both* of you behind the bike-sheds smoking like chimneys!"

"Save your wee-wee! Lover boy! That's if you've got any *left* after extinguishing our cigs!" Natalie jibed relentlessly.

150

"I think we'd be better going *in* now, Nev?" proposed a very composed Candida, *at the same time* tugging his forearm.

"*You do just that!* And *next* time take Miss. Browne, Deputy Head*mistress*, to see *Lady Chatterley*... She can't *wait!*" shouted an increasingly spiteful Mandy to their backs.

The funny thing was: Candida could *afford* to stay *un*provoked because she knew exactly what had eluded both her tormentors: that Ophelia had fulfilled the Date with her sister's enthusiastic backing. Nor would any chance sighting of *Phelia & Nev* let the cat out of the bag - so long as no rumour referenced Candida *in Steve's company* those 5 or 6 miles away.

*****

A good job Candida needed to stay 20 minutes after School that afternoon to discuss the next motion for discussion in Cornfield's Debating Society with the opposing Team Captain. Candida was a spirited & eloquent debater. Outfoxing even Amanda.

In the vacuum of that hold-up, Mandy & Natalie decided they had not quite *finished* with the solitary Neville still in their sights.

"You should have taken *Busy-Izzy* with you! You know how these big girls can devour you *whole*!" warned Mandy: today not *the least bit* protective of - or charitable towards - her former boyfriend.

"*Cradle-snatcher!* That's all she was!" was Natalie's insult, "*mutton dressed up as lamb!*" His tormentor a girl whom even her own foster-mum disliked was now reaching into her quiver for any *extra* arrow to pierce Neville's armour.

"Well I found Ophelia a lot *nicer*, a lot more polite, than I'm finding either of *you*!" was Neville's calm rejoinder, "and to think I ever counted *you* Amanda as my Pal?"

"*And look where it got you*!" rasped Mandy: "boyo now striding out, *in nappies*, in search of a dummy!"

"Hard *luck,* losers!" was Neville's chosen riposte, "You waited till home-time to spout out your bile. It's *you* spoiling for a scrap! Well you're going to be *mighty* disappointed: because Amanda's older brother's already out *and about* to tell her it's her *bed*-time!"

"*Your* bed-time, you mean?" persisted a scowling Natalie, coming to her class-mate Mandy's rescue: "he's put on his 'jamas, *then taken them off again*, with one

Scrubber to his Left, the other Scrubber to his Right! *Whores!"*

With that final put-down, both girls turned down a side-street, giggling away, and *determined* their hilarity would still be heard by a fragile Neville as he kept on along the main road. *The more fragile he: the better.*

FIFTY-TWO

Tuesday was another ordinary school day for Candida : double English Lit., double Geography, single PSE, double History : *not* her favourite day – except it *was* her Birthday.

And like the Queen : she had two Birthdays: one on the actual day, a subdued affair; later on a special treat like a full day at *Alton Towers*, or Scarborough. Birthday Tea today was to be *late*r than usual : 6-30 not 5-15 : best Cheese & Broccoli Quiche - her favourite - plus smoked salmon; and wholemeal rolls filled with everything from prawns to Coronation Chicken.

And guest-of-honour - *were it not she herself?* - was to be Nev: the first time her parents had *properly* had opportunity to get to know Candy's boyfriend.

<<HAPI B/DAY CANDY.MAY C.U.ROUND?WIL B WIV U@ 6.TAKCARE:NEVx>>

"I've brought you a little gift," - he said as he kissed Candida on the cheek - upon her opening the front door at 6-05. Whereupon he dropped a big, brightly-striped, parcel into that same hand - followed by what looked like a box of chocolates, immediately she had deposited the his first prezzy on a nearby hall-stand.

Candida noted straightway that the chocolates [?] were *far* more professionally wrapped than Nev's other gift.

A man's gift-wrapping? Had Nev's stepmother wrapped that *square* box - *even chosen it?* - or had the *Co-operative* Department Store offered to wrap it, after its purchase? Anyway, Candida transported both presents into the lounge, once she'd hung up Nev's green anorak.

Upon entering, his girlfriend tore the envelope away from Nev's card - which was a very serious landscape suitably adorned with two self-stick numbers: a silver'1,' and a little bit wonky gold '9' turned upside down to make '16.' And *there* - seated in front of a hollering Teatime Quiz on the telly - was *Ophelia.*

"Hi, Ophelia !" Neville spluttered, going bright red.

154

"Hello, again!" was the older girl's greeting as she deliberately diverted her eyes anywhere but in his direction.

"Glad you're fully recovered !" Nev said in a voice laden with sympathy : referring to Candida who was still standing watching him to see how he'd react to re-acquaintance with her elder Sister.

Candida now spoke very quickly: *"Of course!* It was only *women's problems."*

"That makes me glad *not* to be a woman." Neville chuckled..

"And thanks for inviting me: *a man*!"

"Boy!" corrected Ophelia. "You're a *boy* till you're in your early 20s..."

"And then they'll call me 'Chap,' 'Mate,' 'Gov,' 'Corporal' : anything but *'ordinary man'*!"

"Better than what some blokes call *us*!" Candida raged: *"'Harlot!', 'Tart!', 'Slut!', 'Bitch!', 'Slag!' "*

Warming to the theme: Ophelia - who was still talking more to the telly than two people there for a joyful

Birthday Bash - added: " 'Cow!', 'Fishwife!', 'Shrew!', 'Floozy!', 'Cuckold!', 'Trollop!' "

"*Gooseberry Fool!*" responded a temporarily-defeated Neville: "I *do* hope *I'm* not the sort of guy who'd use any of those *disgusting* terms!" Their guest could now pat himself on the back that he got the tone of '*disgusting*' right.

"*Good job!*" said Birthday Girl archly, "You'd not be *wel*come here if you so much as *thought* of girls in those terms - never mind *said* it!"

"*I'm not perfect!*" admitted a rather overwhelmed Neville, "Maybe one day I'll have the courage to walk away from such *bravado?*"

"*Bravado?*" Ophelia gasped, just as her mother walked into the Lounge: yet *again* defusing any latent tension with her wonderful timing.

"It's *Mum* you ought to thank for the Invitation, Nev, not *us*," floated Candida, "Our mother *loves* Birthdays! *Except her own!*"

"Very *funny*, Candy!" Mum laughed, before beginning to sing: "*She's just gone Sixteen, going on Seventeen! Who took the Dairy Ice Cream?*"

"She is: a very *young* Sixteen!" Ophelia stressed, after finally using her zapper to silence the telly.

"*Old head on young shoulders*" Neville chipped in: in the forlorn hope such an observation might please *everyone* present.

"I warn you: never, *ever*, try to understand three ladies in a gaggle!" Ophelia clarified for Neville's benefit.

"*You mean three ladies in a giggle?*" quipped Dr. Crabtree who, hungrily, but silently, had appeared through the half-open oak-panelled door.

"*He* should know!" Ophelia cried, "Listen to *him*, Nev! He's an *expert* on managing three ladies."

"Except his Doctorate's in *Psychology*, not *Female* Psychology!" added Candida helpfully.

"*Come on! Let's eat!*" urged the Birthday Girl's Dad, "As it happens, I have got an evening consul*tation* - so will be making polite excuses in about an hour's time."

"On your amazing daughter's biggest *day*?" Candida responded, in mock outrage.

"This is the first day she's allowed to...." continued Ophelia: as if she was going to elaborate on the exact laws of majority.

"*Shut up!*" exclaimed a nonplussed Candida, "if you were about to allude to my first sight of a Bar Parlour: *too late! Been there, done that!*"

"*Holy Saints!*" her father interjected, in mock surprise, "I *think* I'm hearing things I should not be con*doning*?"

"They'll go and do it whether you con-done it *or not!*" responded the girls' Mum with emphasis, "They're never going to tell *us* the full story, nor should they necessarily attempt to?   That's part of growing in*dependent*."

"*I'll drink to that!*" quipped an Ophelia finally rising from her couch, as if healed by Jesus.

FIFTY-THREE

Round the tea-table: a table strewn with a three foot-long silk streamer <<S-I-X-T-E-E-N   T-O-D-A-Y!>> also accompanied by a heart-shaped helium balloon on a wavering stick, emblazoned with a numerical 1-6: both items recently imported from China, Ophelia's mind wandered back 9 days to her Steve's *own* Grand Entrance, VIP invite, to be seated round that same Table.

Then, after the Doctor's simple Grace:

> *" Comes a Birthday Once Again!*
> *Happy Days! Oh Happy Days!*
> *Through the Sunshine & the Rain:*
> *We're Sustained in all our Ways!"*

Candida asked Neville, inquisitively: "And what do *you* normally do for *Izzy's* Birthday?". She didn't know Izzy *well,* but understood she was only a year younger than Neville, brought into his birth home by Dad's new partner Marilyn two years after Neville's *own* mother had disappeared without a lot of warning.

"The Sports' Club where Izzy trains has a special *Events' Room,* and Dad and aims to bring in this commercial Pie-&-Pea firm. *Outsourced!"*

"Well, you're not getting Peas *or* Pies *this evening,*" Eleanor Crabtree informed Neville, "more Keesh Lorraine... and *Salmon.* You *could* say we've killed the fatted *calf* for you... I mean for *the object* of your affections."

Neville's difficulty knowing how to respond - or indeed knowing whether *any* response was required - led Ophelia to rescue the moment: "Perhaps she *is* the fatted calf?"

"*Hell's bells!*" cried Ophelia, her shin suffering a direct hit from her sister's Right foot.

"That wasn't a very *nice* thing to say to your sister on her Special *Day!*" was Mum's delayed response. "Remember in the parable of the *Prodigal Son*, it's the older brother who is jealous when his Dad goes out to meet the renegade, and throws a party for him?" *Here Candy's mother drew on her knowledge of the Bible: references enhanced by her Uncle's calling to the priesthood.*

"Well I'm not jealous of *her!*" Ophelia scorned: "*And* I'm able to rejoice with those who re*joice!*"

"You are *indeed!*" Mum underlined, "and you're usually *kind* to your sister!"- any further faint praise on her part thankfully lost amidst the clatter of every single person round the table taking turns to shovel side of poached salmon, and slices of broccoli-&-mushroom quiche - baby tomatoes, cucumber too - onto best china plates:

a ritual everyone except Neville understood, ensuring nobody missed out on anything.

"I hear you got on very well with Ophelia while her sister was in*disposed.*" Mum said with cheerful smile, this time *expecting* an answer.

"*Very well,* thank you! Mrs. Crabtree," Neville answered, "But I should of course have *loved* Candy to be there as well, I mean instead..." As the Birthday guest fumbled a little, he looked to Ophelia for rescue.

"Yes, we two enjoyed a *very pleasant* evening; my sister, regrettably, *laid aside on a bed of sickness.*"

With jesting now getting out of hand: Mum, Dad and Candida almost swallowed their filled rolls whole, desperately trying to suppress their astonishment at Ophelia's exaggerated reference to *Jairus' daughter.*

William until now, had said little but could resist the temptation to make his contribution no longer: "Yes: when Candy's ill, she's very, *very,* ill. People *do* sympathize with her till they see how speedily she makes a remarkable recovery."

"Listen to the person who calls the doctor out for a *whitlow!*" Candida appealed.

"That's enough, you two!" reprimanded their mother, "I fully expect Neville here will be a lot gentler with his Isobel, than *these* three in their jousting."

"We *do* still have our fall-outs," admitted Neville diplomatically.

"Yes. It's a big change. Can resemble an actual *earthquake*: suddenly, *unexpectedly*, opening your hearth & home to a Step-Sister, or Step-Brother," Dad opined: he privileged to draw on his day-job blending blended families, amalgamating amalgamated families.

"I guess, Doctor Crabtree, me and Izzy soon forget the 'Step' bit," Neville responded without an ounce of confrontation in his clarification: and wise enough not to *lecture* his esteemed host.

Returning to the main subject, Mum stumbled as only one who knew a bit too much behind the scenes could: "Suffice it to say, our Ophelia would have made the best of an unenviable situation, enjoying Friday's film *notwithstanding*."

"It *wasn't* best of a bad Job!" Ophelia protested as she misquoted her mother, "and I don't particularly like that word *'notwithstanding*!' Neville made Friday night very happy! *For both of us!*"

At this juncture, Candida bit her lip, stifling any further observation she might be tempted to make: lest, *accidentally*, she let an extremely feral cat out of the bag so revealing the awful truth *once and for all.*

"Yes, *cometh the moment, cometh the man!*" quoted Dad , perhaps recalling something Sir Walter Scott wrote: at the same time he sensing this round-the-table discussion might be getting less and less celebratory, *more and more tense.*

"Yes: you could call my friend Nev: *a man for all sisters!*" chimed in William, displaying inner pride that he could reclaim the film he'd seen repeated on *Sky*.

After generous helpings, all round, of delicious home-made trifle with cold custard and piped cream, out came a selection of 10 cheeses from *Sainsbury's.*

"Cheshire - or *Stilton*? *Birthday Girl,*" father asked his younger daughter.

"Not so much *'Girl,'* I'm *a woman* now!" Candida reminded everyone, "and *do* pass the *Camembert* too."

"Cheese for you, too, young man ?" Candida's father asked Neville, to which he replied: "A sliver of each, please? You know: you're all *very good* to me?"

Scarcely noticed in this statement was Neville's half smile in the direction of Ophelia: he doubtless hoping he had not said too much. Later that night, he questioned whether there was something deeper going on between himself and Candy's sister: a bond nobody else round that table would - or could - pick up on?

FIFTY-THREE

Back in the lounge, Neville watched Candida open his hastily wrapped *Jigsaw*: a collage of eight royal childhoods; also Marilyn's much neater box of luxury mints. Neville then methodically toured eighteen or nineteen of Candida's *best* Birthday Cards: each given pride-of-place on the marble mantelpiece - before plonking himself down in one of the vacant armchairs.

Duly seated, he turned to Candida again: "You know it was very *good* of you to lend your sister to me while you were so unwell. Ophelia made me feel so *included* - when otherwise I would have been all on my ownio!"

And before the younger sister had any chance to speculate further on how well the swop had, or had not, gone, Ophelia spoke out: " I'm not a *Library* Book, issued because '*Just William*' has gone out on someone else's ticket! I wouldn't have subbed for Candy unless I *wanted* to."

"You wanted to because it was *Nev*! – and you were *curious*, Phelia: *curious*! You wanted to approve my choice!" Candida needled, warming to the discussion.

"And *FAME* the film is *brilliant!*" Ophelia waxed lyrical, "worth every penny of the three-pound School Child concession!"

"You *a School Child*! Talk about *flukes?*" exclaimed Candida with incredulity.

"Yes I'm so chuffed to be counted *anybody's* choice. I mean I wouldn't be everybody's choice. *Izzy's* the better bargain in our household!" Neville added with genuine modesty.

"If it wasn't my Birthday, I'd send you back home double*quick*, young *man!*" cried a conceivably injured Candida, "right back to the cave you *came* from*!* All this talk about '*Bargains*'! Maybe my dear sister's *right*? We're *not* second-hand wardrobes."

"But we do *borrow* from each other's wardrobe, second-hand *or not*!" Ophelia pointed out: all the while stirring the pot ever more vigorously.

"And I always...." - but before Candida could reply to her sister's woefully prolonged joke, Neville attempted to introduce a bit of sanity: "You both look super *whatever* you're wearing - *borrowed or not*! Our Izzy would look *great* in such vivid colours!"

"And she'll *thank* you for telling her" was Candida's acid advice to her boyfriend.

"Well you won't see *me* in Purple anytime soon - *or Mustard*!" protested Ophelia, "there's no accounting for *some people's* taste?"

"Don't listen to *her*, Nev!" Candida commanded. "She's a Dowd!"

"I'm *not* a..."

"Perhaps *she* - I mean *Ophelia* - wants to look more studious, dressed more like for the *office*?" poor Neville argued: he blissfully unaware that any boy daring to judge women's fashion would likely be obliterated.

Mercifully, at this potentially awkward moment, Mum breezed in for a third time and asked them to join in a final: "*Happy Birthday to you!*" before Dad went off to his evening Clinic.

At this, both girls, in unison, sighed impatiently. Even so, Ophelia *still* felt she ought to join in an increasingly raucous rendering of that dreadfully trite ditty: made worse, this time, by Willie stretching, in descant, the third line: "*Happy, Birthday Dear C-A-A-A-N-D-Y!*" so professionally as to threaten to undermine the whole exercise.

Luckily for him, nobody *except* Neville appeared to notice: he winking at his mate in unfettered appreciation.

"And I must be going too!" Neville announced, "I have *far* extended my welcome."

As he pecked the younger sister's cheek a second time that evening, the older girl further down the downstairs' passage resisted the temptation to agree with him: "Yes you *have!*"

_____

ΩΨΩΨΩΨΩΨΩΨΩΨΩ

FIFTY-FOUR

Ophelia wasn't *really* close to Penelope: who disliked the name 'Penny' unless in the mouth of someone really, really, *family*. Yet Penelope - a tall, intelligent and self-assured Sixth-former- was certainly in Ophelia's friendship-group: each girl able to pool frustrations and to pool triumphs without letting each other down. Nor ever *telling* their respective parents how different girls, indigenous daughters too, marked their parent-craft!

So Penelope was *definitely* someone to take notice of. Privily, all her teachers agreed the same!

"Phelia?" Penelope inquired the Wednesday after the swop, as both girls sat at a opposite ends of the same table in the School Library before afternoon lessons, "Is it true you spent *part* of Friday evening with a lad from *Year 11?"*

"Why do you ask?" queried Ophelia, her voice betraying tiny offence: "happens all the time! I know mothers 5 years older than fathers; fathers *15* years older than mothers! Also two women living together, aged *50* and *70. What's the big deal?"*

"The *'deal'* as you put it, Phelia, is that two-and-a-bit years is a really big gap in the Upper-Sixth. And you did *worse* than choosing a Year 11 pupil; you chose a Year 11 lad *going out with your own sister*!"

"Seeing you're so *inter*ested, Pen: there's quite a simple explanation," Ophelia continued: "Candy had period pains and sent me to meet Nev instead! *Satisfied*?"

"Sorry! Shouldn't have put you through the third degree. *I* have period pains, *really bad!* I still wouldn't ask Alice, the girl next door, to go and meet my bloke. What might she get *up to*? These things happen - even though Alice is as *honest* as the night is long."

"*Glad to hear she is!*" responded Ophelia tartly: "and whoever asks you, Counsellor: Candy considered *me* to be reliable! Though we do have our *occasional* differences..."

"*Occasional?*" Penelope chortled.

"Actually, I had a *good* evening: giving Candy ample chance to nurse her tummy! Also Nev had a dollop of company: *my* company! It's ten-to-two. *Let's go to History!*"

As the two Year 13s crossed the quadrangle, Penelope brought out her trump card. "Natalie *Parsons* is spreading the word that you were snogging Neville!"

"*Little scoundrel!*" snarled Ophelia: "I wouldn't trust anything Natalie *Parsons* says! *Ever!* She hates my *guts*: because I got her some Detentions. Punishment justified on *all three* occasions!"

"So you *didn't* snog Neville?"

"Don't be *stu*pid, Pen! You know me well enough to understand I'd only ever be *civil* to someone else's sweetheart: first, '*Hello!*'; later. '*Goodbye!*'..." Here Ophelia was anxious to put the record straight, while *not* sounding defensive.

"Hello!; then *Goodbye!*" Penelope dutifully repeated: she inwardly still unsure she had heard *everything*?

And so to Class.

FIFTY-FIVE

"*Hi, Nev!*" Candida, on foot, welcomed Neville, also on foot, from an opposite direction.

To-night, the younger sister was *not* dressed for posh Art Galleries - yet nevertheless looked stunning in bright red tee-shirt tucked into tight navy trousers. "I didn't get chance between classes to compliment you on your soldierly reaction to the Mandy's *muckraking* and her sidekick Natalie's poison. *I was really proud of you!*"

"And I'm proud of *you*, Candy!" responded Neville with enthusiasm, "remember it's *you* who stuck up for *me*!"

"*Easy to do!*" Candida kept to the subject, "because you're *hon-our-able*! and very *depend-able*!"

"Thanks! *You too!*" Here Neville kept up an interchange far more positive than anything achieved on his girlfriend's birthday: "That's what *drew* me to you, just when I thought you'd turn me *down*?"

"Well you thought *wrong!*" Candy stressed. "I've had plenty of time to observe your treatment of women - even if you *did* go out with that scumbag Mandy!" By now Candida was as animated as she was non-confrontational with her lover-boy.

ΩΨΩΨΩΨΩΨΩΨΩΨΩΨΩ

FIFTY-SIX

After a walk round the Park, along to the Shops, Candida and Neville landed up inside a traffic-island *Burger-Bar* difficult, *if not impossible*, to access on foot.

Wrong choice?

Gloria Starcross was seated at a neighbouring table with Stan and Bob from Year 10, one year *below* Candida & Nev's Year 11.

"*Gosh!* A different *girlie* to-night?" Gloria taunted, allowing a hostile Bob to add: "*Good on yer*, Mister. Doing the *Milk* Round are you? Didn't you *know* they're all drawn to that wench like piranhas?"

"*Sorry,* I don't follow...?" Nev began his apologia: before a seemingly far *kinder* Stan intervened: "*Keep quiet, Bob!* Remember where you *are!* In other words, give the poor chappie a *break!* If he fancies Head *Prefects,* that's up to *him* - provided he's not caught smoking behind the *bike*-shed! And so long as he washes his Y-fronts in *Omo!*"

Before Neville - *or Candida* - could decide whether Stan's stance was supportive or not, Gloria Starcross stood up, beckoning her companions: "*Time to go!* Let's leave them to their *crump*ets! ....*Cheeri-bye folks!*"

"*Good riddance!*" Neville growled beneath his breath: "I *do* hope that hasn't *spoilt* your evening?"

"*Not at all!*" replied Candida with conviction, "Veggie Burger with small fries, beans, and diet coke, please... and *no* sauces..."

Ten minutes of patient queueing later, Neville returned with laden tray to find three gold *coins* on his place-mat.

"Candy I don't *want* that! I've done a *car* wash!"

"Well if *I* were you, I'd stuff it in your pocket, but take it out before Izzy's on hand with her *OMO!*" By now the two were both choking with laughter.

And how they *stayed.* Stayed and chatted about Candida's Birthday, already 3 days since; about Izzy's training régime; her trophies; also Marilyn's skill assisting everyone with their French *Home*work... *and* Scotch new-boy *Sam.*

ΩΨΩΨΩΨΩΨΩΨΩΨΩ

FIFTY-SEVEN

That same Friday, Ophelia was early off a longer Bus-ride to meet Steve.

"*Hello again!*" she said a little shyly, as his car drew up into a nearby lay-by."

"Hope you've got a good appetite! For I wanted to take you to *The Florentine*: a treat you missed through your illness."

"Through my *period* pains," clarified Ophelia; a bolt-upright Steve holding his car door open for her to sit and reach for her seat-belt. "*Thanks again!* I'm sure *The Florentine* will match the bill?"

"It did last *Friday!*" Steve enthused. "Candida was really *special* company. It was so sweet of you to send her in your stead! She's so *bubbly*! Such *splendid* company!"

"*Hope I am too?*" Ophelia responded sharply. "I've evidently got big *shoes* to fill!"

"Just be *yourself*! That's order of the day," Steve advised more than a little condescendingly as he swung round again to *open* the door for his regular companion.

Nobody can ascertain, at this particular point of this anticlimactic Friday evening, whether Steve is finding Ophelia's black trouser-suit quite as alluring as her sister's bright yellow frock 164 hours or so previous.

FIFTY-EIGHT

On their way home - Neville never left Candida to do it on her own, even on a midsummer afternoon - he slowed down beneath the sycamore tree opposite *Southlands primary School*: "Can I kiss you Good-*night*?" he asked really hesitantly, even nervously, "*properly?*"

"That's a change of *routine!*" replied a faintly astonished Candida. "It's normally me asking *you!*"

"Well I haven't wanted to lose you by pestering you: by being too *fro*-ward?" Yes. Neville was quite pleased with this Elizabethan(?) anachronism.

"No danger of *that*! Well, *come on!*" Candida teased, pouting her lips into an 'O' shape as encouragement for Nev to imitate her 'O' with an 'O' of his own.

But this parting of the ways was *different*. Candida could feel his tongue pressing on her only-slightly-unlocked teeth: pressing till spontaneously the tip of his tongue met the tip of hers.

"Henry VIII be *confounded*!" Candida spluttered: "What's got *into* you? Must have been some hefty-spiced *Cheese*burger? Usually you're as stitched *up* as a Carthusian Monk!"

"Sorry!"

"Sorry? Silly *boy!* You needn't be sorry! Do it *again!*"

Neville still appeared a fraction reluctant. In fact he looked *all round* to check whether Amanda or Natalie or Tom or Stanley or Robert - or *Samuel* - were looking.

This time, Candida's tongue was not held quite so resolutely behind clenched teeth. Instead, Nev's own tongue revolved round and round hers - but only for four or five revolutions.

This time it was a startled *Candida* who spoke first: "Somebody's been *teaching* you!" she chided.

"No it just came *naturally*...Be*lieve* me!" stumbled Neville, afraid now to look Candy straight in her eyes.

"It didn't *feel* as if it was entirely spon*taneous*!" Here Candida sensed she was onto something.

However her persistent questioning of him didn't translate to a faintly embarrassed Neville as either hostile *or* angry. Simply that his escort was *dumbfounded*.

Perhaps he was anxious not to betray Ophelia to her younger sister? So he quivered like a floating leaf.

"Stop *worry*ing, Stupid!" Candida ordered, incidentally coming to her boyfriend's *rescue*: "I might *hate* Phelia some days - *most days?* - and wish she'd never been *born*: but one thing I'll never get at her for - if it *was* her? - is teaching you naughty *kissing*!"

"Candy, are you *sure*?" an amazed Neville stuttered.

"Of course I'm sure*, idiot*! ... And while we're *talking* about secrets, I went to Vanessa's sleep-over this time last year. It was part of her Mum & Dad's Birthday Present to her. Nothing *bad* happened, but when the lights went out, Nessa offered to teach *me* kissing the French way. And I enjoyed it! *Too much!*"

"Enjoyed it? A *girl* doing it aged only *15*? *Surely not*?" gasped Neville as he covered his mouth.

"Yes girls *do* kiss each other!" Candida chuckled.

"But not like *that*! *Surely not?* Izzy would never think of kissing another *girl*."

"Don't be too cock-sure, Nev! Give her a couple more years and she'll be coming off that podium and *hugging* whichever two girls came second and third."

"But not like....?"

"Come on, Nev. The Party's *over*! *Bedtime*!" Candida now tugged his limp hand ever more urgently.

"So I haven't got your Ophelia *into trouble*?"

"Gracious me, Nev! *Someone* had to tell you how to do it- so it might as well be *Phelia* : while I was indis*posed*."

Silence. "Hope she liked it as much as I did?" Candida joked - *or was there a hint of sarcasm in her speculation?*

Neville could not tell. But if Candy *said* her older sister wasn't going to be hung, drawn and quartered, he had to take the effervescent Candida at her word?

FIFTY-NINE

"Signor! *Signora!*" was Marco 's ostentatious greeting as he stretched to open the door of his restaurant for both his prize Patrons to enter. *"No coat, Madam?"*

"No coat to-night! Balmy *breezes,*" Ophelia assured the Maître, he with coat-hangers to the fore.

"And shall you be wanting *a quiet table*?" Marco fussed.

"Far *in!*" "*Quite* quiet!" both Patrons talked over each other.

A moment later, Marco was drawing a chair back for Ophelia, and smoothing a stiffly-starched Egyptian-cotton serviette on her lap. "An apéritif for Madam?"

"Actually, a small sherry's fine!"

"And blackcurrant & lemon for *you,* Sir ?"

"*Plus* a litre of sparkling water," Steve methodically added.

Five minutes later, the unctuous Marco reappeared: "I *do* hope Madam's full health is restored. Relieved to be up and *about* again?"

"I'm not his *wife,* you know, Signor! I'm Ophelia *Crabtree,*" Steve's guest stressed, with not a little annoyance.

"Yes, I know the good Lady who accompanied Sir, *last* Friday, did the gentleman - *and* herself - credit under such *sad* circumstances. It was a pleasure to be at her *service!*" Marco gushed, totally unaware he was ruffling even *more* feathers.

"*Pleasure!*" Ophelia hissed under her breath.

"I'll be back in five minutes to take Madam's order"

"Make that *ten!*" Ophelia requested.

And as soon as this obsequious Presence had disappeared to welcome another two Guests, Ophelia turned and looked Steve right in the eye: "Putting all the flowers and your *handkerchief* to one side, did you *really* enjoy my sister's company?" she probed.

A trifle evasively, even haughtily, Steve replied: "*Nothing*, Dear, could possibly compensate me for *your* absence. It's such a relief this evening that we're back on track... *and together*. Together for what should be an *outstanding* eating experience?"

"*Outstanding* it probably was for my stand-in," Ophelia observed coldly.

"Don't jump to conclusions... What I like *most* about this amazing establishment is its freedom from urgency or distraction. With no *tele*phones!" Here Steve - *guided solely by diplomacy?* - attempted to change the subject.

"Except for *text*ing ?" was Ophelia's qualification to this *Florentine* prohibition: "In fact now I've decided on Haddock Chowder and Ravioli I guess I could text Candida *now*?" The older sister was now purposefully provocative.

"Or perhaps *not*?" suggested a somewhat baffled Steve, "She might not *welcome* any interruption of her own evening out with Neville - if that young man is fortunate enough *still* to be her Courtier?"

"*Still her Courtier*," Ophelia repeated over and again, "still her Courtier."

Steve's 'Madam' rather enjoyed such an antique description of a lad known to everybody else as one of the most informal scholars you could possibly meet. *And she of all people knew a great deal more about Candy's selection.*

181

Then, only briefly put off by Steve passing on her order to an equally solicitous waiter - black rubber apron down to his ankles - Ophelia ostentatiously tapped the keys of her silenced phone:

<< C-a-n-d-y! H-a-r-d a-c-t 2 f-o-l-l-o-w? A-t F-l-o-r-e-n-t-i-n-e!!! L-o-v-e 2 N-e-v! O x >>

SIXTY

Candida was still earlier than Ophelia getting in. In fact, as she turned her cheapo phone on, at the bottom of the stairs, she found 2 messages not one in her Inbox.

On running home so as not to worry Marilyn overmuch, Nev had texted:

<< HI!LIKD2NITE!!URSOGOOD4ME!SLEEPWEL!NXXX>>

And as she emerged from the Guest bathroom, Candida again saw her brother's light on.

"Can I come *in*?" she asked William without giving him any opportunity to say 'No!'

"I've had a fab evening with Nev. Fancy: he knew *you* before he knew *me*! All except that 'orrible Gloria & her two tow-rags, Stan & *Bob*! Have *you* ever come across them, Willie?"

"*Vaguely*," he answered, "being a year behind me, they're more *names* than people to me. Not pals. They say Bob's *brilli*ant on the Trampoline! That's maybe why he hangs out with that Stan who's not really good at *any*thing?"

"Surely he must be good at *something*? Fishing? Boxing? Running errands?" Candida queried as she prodded her brother's leg through the bed-clothes, so she'd be a little more comfortable.

"The only errand *he'll* ever run will be with Weed in his pocket!" William suggested with some feeling, "and as for *Gloria*, I think even her *Mum* must say she's mixing with the wrong types!"

"Thanks for filling me in, Willie! *Lights off?*"

"In a minute: when I've finished this Chapter. A real *cliff-hanger* this!"

"Well, let's hope whoever it is doesn't fall *off* the cliff!" Candida lamented.

"*Wait for next week's thrilling episode!*" was her 'little' brother's quotation from '*The T.V.Times.*'

" And *thanks,* Willie, for being so, *so,* careful not telling the *full* story of last week's swop. *Without* you, we'd be *done for*! *Sleepie-tighty!*"

SIXTY-ONE

On the morning of the Friday before Autumn Half-Term- an *Inset* day for teacher training - an *un*scheduled Steve was knocking on the knocker before the family had even finished their breakfast.

"*Hello* Mrs. *Crab*tree!" he spluttered upon *Clovelly*'s heavy front-door being opened on its chain, "I've got something for Candida: a late *Birthday* present! I ordered it on *Amazon* - and it's *arrived* now... and I *do* want her to have it before she's seventeen - not 16."

"Well, you'd better come *in*, Steve. I'll just check that Candida's *decent.*

"Yes she *is*! Here she *is*!" Candida's mother assured their visitor who had not progressed much further than the hall-stand. "But don't be too *long,* as my husband always likes to drive to Wales fairly *early*. And we're not *quite* ready.

Steve didn't have chance to reply before a vaguely surprised Candida came along the passage and sat on the solitary seat provided for guests. Self-consciously, and hastily, Candida folded her towelling dressing-gown over her bare legs and shiny knees.

"I've so *wanted* this parcel to arrive!" said the man in *Armani* shirt and striped *St. Cuthbert's Old Boys'* tie. "But it came in stapled cardboard. So I took the liberty of taking out and wrapping it *properly.*"

"That's very *kind* of you, Steve, but your Birthday *Card* was quite enough."

However, before a clearly embarrassed, and still underdressed, Candida could object, Steve strode forward and plonked a *very* heavy parcel on her towelled lap.

Gingerly, the younger girl tugged at the over-sellotaped blue foil wrapping: her first vain attempts at wrenching the foil undone coinciding with *Ophelia*'s appearance behind her.

185

"Good Morning, *Steve!*" was Ophelia's rather cool welcome, "What a sur*prise*! And all for Candy's 16th. *birthday?*"

But her man-friend was already too engrossed following *Candida's* every movement to reply.

At last an enormous tome slipped out of the far end of Candida's heavy parcel on to the carpeted floor. And there was still airtight *cellophane* to tackle before her access to the main prize.

"*ITALY : One Thousand Years of History, Culture & Art,*" Candida read out the title slowly. "*Stephen*, there must be some *mistake*? Surely this is for *Phelia* not me!"

"No, *no!*" Steve disputed: "Definitely for *you,* Candida: because it fell to you, so clearly, so candidly, to be so intrigued by, so immersed in, the Country we now know as *Italy* - while your sister was so *ill.*"

If, perchance, this daybreak visitor con*grat*ulated himself on a similarly sounding 'Candida'-'Candid': all likes, or likenesses, went over the two girls' heads.

"*Indisposed*! *Not* ill," Ophelia insistently corrected Steve, "and can I say on Candy's behalf how much she

186

appreciates such a *delightful* Birthday Gift: a tribute to her very wide-ranging interests and preoccupations. A real *Culture-Vulture* if ever there *was* one!"

"*Something* like that?" an unimpressed Candida limply responded.

"And now, *if you don't mind*, Stephen, *you* need to go to your employ, leaving *us* to get ready for *Wales*. We'll ring! *Good day!*" Here Ophelia could scarcely have sounded *less* frosty were the corridor thermostat to register minus 10°.

And just in case an abashed, rather *crestfallen*, Steve needed any further elucidation of his girlfriend's indignation, he had only to note Ophelia's alacrity to slam the door behind him.

No sweetness and light on this occasion from *either* of the sisters he'd taken to meet Marco at *The Florentine*.

SIXTY-TWO

Seated in folding chairs next to each other on the *Monday* of their week of caravanning in Wales: both women taking advantage of surprisingly warm October

elevenses - Eleanor Crabtree leaned forward : *"Candida,
I just wanted to take the chance of all the others
walking to the village shop to ask what you *really* think
about the big Experiment, your swop? *Do* tell me!"*

"But you know the rules we set ourselves: '*No* inquests!'
'*No* analysis!' '*No* regrets!' '*No* recriminations!' "
Candida recited: "far better *that* way: then *nobody* is
hurt?"

"*Hurt* is a very strong word," Eleanor picked up
straightway her daughter's prevarication: "Your father
and me: we feared there *could* be *down*sides - but did
not willingly want to stand in your *way*, because you
both needed vali*dation*?"

"You mean we were unknowingly sitting on *doubts*?"
Candida checked out.

"*Good Heavens, Candy! Everyone* has doubts when they
fall in love!" mother now at her most sickly-sweet,
"more doubts perhaps at the *start* of a friendship than
basking in its *maturity. Mind you?* There are thousands
of divorces: couples splitting right into their 70s!"

"Jumping ahead a bit *aren't we*?" observed a subdued -
and astonished - Candida: "neither me *nor* Phelia is
even thinking of *marriage* - let alone di*vorce*!"

188

"I'm sure you're not!" responded the girls' mother soothingly, "In fact I'm *glad* you're not!"

Silence.

"School love it shouldn't happen - but what happens when it does?" Now Eleanor achieved the seemingly unachievable - and released all the tension.

"Glad you *like* that song, Mum!" Candida smiled, "Phelia introduced it to me from an old *Grange Hill* record."

"So perhaps I shouldn't *probe?*" the parted girl's inquisitor asked, "and I *certainly* shouldn't conduct a post-*mortem!*"

Another silence.

"But I want you to *know* I'm around to listen if you ever discover Neville's *diff*erent from what you expected? Or when you're going through a rough patch." *Here the mother clinging onto her casebook for dear life.*

"*Thank*you, Mum, but I don't *do* rough patches!" Candida suddenly became spirited. "What happens, *happens*! Who falls by the wayside, falls. And I *for one* have no regret *whatsoever* about our Experiment!"

"Good! That's *good*, dearest!" close of Subject, at least to Eleanor's satisfaction, if not Donald's: the two routinely tipping each other off. "Now for the *runner-beans*! We'll soon have 3 hungry *warriors* joining us!"

This degree of expectancy prompted Candida to scan the Camp highway repeatedly, in search of possible customers.

"Sing along to *string* along!" her mother hummed whilst a faintly baffled Candy gripped her potato-peeler ever tighter.

SIXTY-THREE

Walking round Lake Bala - *just the two of them* - on the *Wednesday* of their Half-Term holiday, Mum was *determined* to button-hole *Ophelia*.

Taking this opportunity presented little risk, she reasoned, as her 'little chat' with Candida two days earlier had gone so well that - *even if Candy had reported their exchange straight back to Phelia* - nothing would be lost.

"Did you *enjoy* the swop: your swop with Candida?" her elder daughter's mother asked innocently.

" Yes! *Why do you ask?*" Ophelia answered defensively, "both of us, I mean *all three* of us, if you include Little Willie, agreed we would rouse no questions, put to bed no answers! ...And that's worked fairly well, *so far...*"

In her perspicacity, honed & fine-tuned over 22 years of marriage to a Psychologist, Ophelia's mother grasped those two words *'so far'* and probed further: "Of course, of *course*! You and Candy *do* seem to have ridden wild waves effortlessly. You're actually being *polite* to each other!" *Here she chuckled.*

"Don't be like that!" exclaimed a slightly offended Ophelia, "there *are* days when we get on each other's nerves - *which 2 girls so near in age wouldn't?* - but Candy's heart's in the right place!"

"You're as generous as ever, *dearest*!" Mum now complimented Phelia, "you trusted Candida with Steve - and it could be that trust in her, *that trust in him*, might, *or might not*, have been misplaced? And potentially, *your sister*'s trust in your boyfriend might, *or might not*, be shallower than you *imagine*? "

Now it was *Ophelia*'s turn to pick up on one single word: *"'Misplaced*?' *Of course not! No way!* Whatever made you think he - *or she* - would act like *wrecking*-balls?"

Ophelia was quite pleased with a word-picture borrowed from the demolition of buildings.

"Of course! *Of course, darling!*" Mum spoke reassuringly: "Of course everyone was on their *best behaviour! The only way in the circumstances?*"

"I wouldn't go quite as far as *that!*" was Ophelia's perspective. "Steve's *always* on his best behaviour. Very old-*fashioned*. Very *precise!*"

Silence.

"Now can we talk about something *else*?"

SIXTY-FOUR

Friday, December 20th., 2002

Only three weeks beforehand, the two girls had decorated the *'Penthouse'* with a artificial tree, all silver;

lots of baubles; many lengths of tinsel; and a rather naff 3-foot long gold-foil fringe announcing:

<<M-E-R-R-Y C-H-R-I-S-T-M-A-S ! >>:

all these festoons *sparkling* due to an additional string of 36 fairly cheap fairy-lights Ophelia had picked up in *Wilko.*

"Don't electrocute yourselves!" was her father's warning when Candida attached said lights to an already over-burdened socket: the socket some people call *'A plug.'* Meaning *plug-hole*?

But midst all this glitter, on this particular afternoon, the first day of *Alderman Cornfield's* Christmas Holiday, here was Ophelia in floods *of tears.* And it wasn't because it was *her* turn to vacuum the lounge and the stairs.

And quite spontaneously, Candida put her arms round her sister's shoulders: *"What's wrong?"*

"I've *finished* with Steve! *Finished!"* Ophelia wept.

"Finished ? What do you *mean*, Phelia?" Candida now stretched a Left arm to grab two more big tissues from the huge box of *Kleenex for Men* Phelia kept on her bedside table. *These not refused. Nor* a clutch of three further tissues 5 minutes later.

And at that crucial moment, *William* knocked on their door and came in to show them his latest *Airfix* model: a *Seafire,* to celebrate the 60th. Anniversary of its sea-to-air service in the *2nd. World War.*

"Have I come at the wrong time?" he asked: he tactfully glancing away from his older sister Ophelia with her blotched cheeks, "I shouldn't have said how my big sister's Stollen Cake you made was *a bit dry!"*

"Perhaps come back another time, Willie?" Candida smiled: "then we can both admire your *Spitfire,* or whatever, *properly."*

Then - just as her brother was retreating through a still slightly ajar door - Candy added, *reassuringly:* "This is nothing to *do* with the *Stollen!* I, *too,* found my few mouthfuls a bit hard-*going!"*

SIXTY-FIVE

"Candy, it's *over!* And I once felt I was so *lucky!"*

"You *were* lucky, Phelia," Candida agreed, her Left arm now migrating to her sister's waist. "And I had a *splendid* time with Steve that Friday evening! On our swop! Him so *generous*! And so *cultured!*"

"I'm certain you did - and *relieved* you did!" bawled the older sister, "that's the *trouble!*"

"Sorry I don't *follow* you, Phelia? When I said 'I': I mean *we* - had a splendid time, I only meant *varied* - & *expensive!*" Candida recalled: "There was *no* hanky-panky! You know I'd *never* betray you!"

"*So you say*, Candy. I *hear* what you say! But I've often wondered *in the back of my mind* what really *did* take place that evening I was ill - I mean when that evening I was *well?*"

At this point, Ophelia seemed, to her concerned sister, to perk up a little.

"But we said from the *start*: 'No *Inquests*,' 'No En*quiring*,' - and I think we've *kept* to that," added Candida gently, " We were *all* committed to keep it that way. Perhaps *too* committed?"

"On that account, true!" a still upset Ophelia blubbered: "You've been *marvellous*, Candy! *So discreet!*"

"I wouldn't go *that* far!" the Comforter now sounded a trifle hesitant: "there have been times when I've been tempted to cross-question you, *and* Nev! ... And I've been so *irritated* by his stupid texts, I've almost thrown my phone down *the stairs!*"

"Candy: you've *nailed* it! *Phones!*" Candy's sister suddenly found enlightenment. "Yesterday evening, *after* the Concert, I picked up Steve's phone *by accident*: perhaps *not* by accident? And I wasn't too happy with what I *found!*"

"*Surely* Sis! Surely, you wouldn't look at Steve's phone when he wasn't *there*? *Wicked!*" Candida had not lost her capacity for astonishment.

"Well I *shouldn't* scan his phone, but I *did!*" admitted the now less tearful, more *defiant*, older sister. "When Steve stopped off outside his flat to fetch me that box of *Black Magic*: that *pre*-Christmas Christmas present he'd half-promised me- but then forgot to bring with him: *that's* when I looked at his phone!"

"*Naughty!*" Candida again reproved Ophelia without much conviction. "Anyway, how could you find the right button, the right page, under such *time*-pressure?"

"I did - because he'd put the chocs in a hiding-place he couldn't find! And what *I* found were a dozen or so photos of *you*, Candy!" Phelia spluttered between a bout of renewed tears: "*You* in bright yellow dress outside this Gallery. You in the same yellow dress outside that Italian Restaurant. You in yellow dress, back view. Worse: you as a *baby*. You in your school *uniform*, Year 10. You next to *William* at his Boy Scout Awards. You on Sports' Day: the time you won the 400 metres *when nobody expected you to!*"

"*Never!* I don't *believe* it," responded Candida: "I've got some vague memory of that servile Chef, *Marco*, offering to take a photo of us both together; and Divinia at the Gallery joining us for a photo-opp after her speech, but *nothing* else. I can only think your Steve took some photos - *stole some photos* - when he came for Tea that Sunday. When neither of us were *looking*? I mean me in my school *uniform*! *Creepy!*"

"*Yes*, come to think of it, he was away for 6 or 7 minutes on the toilet... said he'd got constipation after not eating since *Breakfast*!" recalled Ophelia. "That must have been when he *did* it: photographing our family's photos in their frames, *close to*!"

"And *his* camera-phone would be a lot posher than my pay-as-you-go *Tesco reject*!" Here Candida would have grinned had that not been the wrong mood-music. "Try photographing even the outside of *Buckingham Palace* with *mine?*"

SIXTY-SIX

"Well I held my *nerve*! *And* I held my *tongue*!" Ophelia continued her re-telling the previous evening's saga with a note of accomplishment, *almost victory*, in her voice, "I wasn't going to *own up* to retrieving his Photo-Archive. And I certainly wasn't going to let him see me *upset*! "

"Maybe Steve wanted a photo of that *too*?" Candida suggested, "*Phelia the Fallible*?"

"Anyway, I told him to drive me straight *home*!" continued Ophelia as realistically as if Steve was with them upstairs at that exact minute. "And whatever his sugar-sweet *sycophancy*, I told him I wasn't in the *mood* to *prolong* the evening after such a boring, squeaky, *repetitive*, Concert. Fancy all *three* separate High School Orchestras rehearsing, worse *performing*, allegedly brilliant medleys of Christmas Carols - *including that horrible 'Jingle Bells'* - without *telling* each other?"

"So how *did* you break the news to him, about your *finishing* like with him?" asked the younger sister.

"*This* is how I did it: when he drew up outside the house, I thanked him for the mints, but said I didn't fancy seeing him *ever again!*"

"Gordon *Bennett!* You sure held your *nerve!*"

"Yes I said the end of an old year was as good a time as any to end things..." By now Ophelia's relaying of the tale was beginning to falter again: *still too raw?*

Candy, surprised, checked out she had *heard* it right: "Steve accepted it that *meekly?*"

"He had no *choice!*" Ophelia rasped, "he looked a bit downcast, and started as if he was going to ask me supplementary questions. Then he *dared* to say 'I'd feel different in the *morning!*' But the way I turned my back on him and *slammed* the passenger door behind me, I *think* - I *hope-* he got the *message!*"

"And to imagine I knew nothing about all this - though I *might* have had a *teeny-weeny* suspicion? - till just now!" Candida confessed.

Awkward silence.

"And it's *me* who split you up?" Candida speculated, with a huge portion of contrition. Lack of *weeping* on the younger girl's part *might,* however, have been recognition that she herself *hadn't* acted naïvely, nor led the older man *on. Far from it!* On the spur of the moment, she convinced herself that she had been almost rude, *resisting* Stephen's clumsy advances?

"No, Candy! It's not *you* who's caused this: this parting of the ways," wailed Ophelia, "*not at all!* That's plain for *all* to see! You were just in the right place at the wrong time; or in the wrong place at the right time - or in the wrong place at the wrong time.... when I was *ill!*"

"*Ill!*"

"What's *more,* Candy," here the older sister regained some of her composure: "you've helped to bring something *to the surface* that otherwise would have remained *hidden*? One man's *infatuation!*"

"An obsession I became subject of - the *object* of? - by so willingly going ahead with the *swop*?" Candida persisted.

"*No!* How many times do I have to *tell* you, *Silly*?" Ophelia chided her sister, "Our swop only brought all this *to the surface*! A lot of those photographs Steve took, *including* the ones he possesses 'to remember his *Tea-with-the-Crabtrees*,' pre-*date* our Experiment."

"You mean Steve courted *you*, Phelia, when all along he really wanted to court *me*?" For a second or third time, Candy sought clarification, "*Loopy!* Completely *barmy!*"

"*True!*" the older girl spoke with some sadness, "This episode teaches us that ev'ry man in this world must take con*trol* of his own feelings - *and his own Lust!*"

"*Lust*?" Candida now sounded energized enough to get her tongue fully round a word that sounded so like it really was. "*Lust!*"

"Yes, lascivious *Lust!*" repeated Ophelia, patiently. "It was all right for him to *like* you; and it was all right for him to like your yellow *dress*. And it was all right for you to *wear* that yellow dress: even if it would *not* have been my *own* choice!"

Here Candida held back from saying: "I know all *about* your taste in dress!" *instead* commenting: "Yes that was the *real* me! The *real* me that Friday evening.... And it turns out Steve had motives, *designs*, I couldn't get my *head* round. Except odd *glimpses*..."

"Glimpses not for *you* to fathom but for him to confront, him to *un*-fathom!" counselled Ophelia, *finally letting logic triumph over her grief?*

"So you're not blaming *me* for your predicament - I mean for *his* misbehaviour?" asked Candida with relief.

"*No blame* - no condemnation - *at all,* Candy! And I shall *never* hold this against you. In fact I'll try to make *your* Christmas as happy as mine will be. *Without him!*"

"That's very *kind* of you, Sis! I don't *deserve* you!"

"You *do*! *And more!*" Ophelia glowed - as she screwed up all eleven sodden tissues and tossed them in the bin.

ΘΘΘΘΘΘΘΘΘΘΘΘΘΘ